GEEK GÎRL

GEEK DRAMA

Photograph © Geor

Holly Smale is the author of *Geek Girl*, *Model Misfit*, *Picture Perfect* and *All That Glitters*. She was unexpectedly spotted by a top London modelling agency at the age of fifteen and spent the following two years falling over on catwalks, going bright red and breaking things she couldn't afford to replace. By the time Holly had graduated from Bristol University with a BA in English Literature and an MA in Shakespeare she had given up modelling and set herself on the path to becoming a writer.

Geek Girl was the number-one bestselling young-adult fiction title in the UK in 2013. It was shortlisted for several major awards including the Roald Dahl Funny Prize and the Branford Boase award, nominated for the Queen of Teen Award and won the teen and young adult category of the Waterstones Children's Book Prize and the 11–14 category of the Leeds Book Award.

www.facebook.com/geekgirlseries

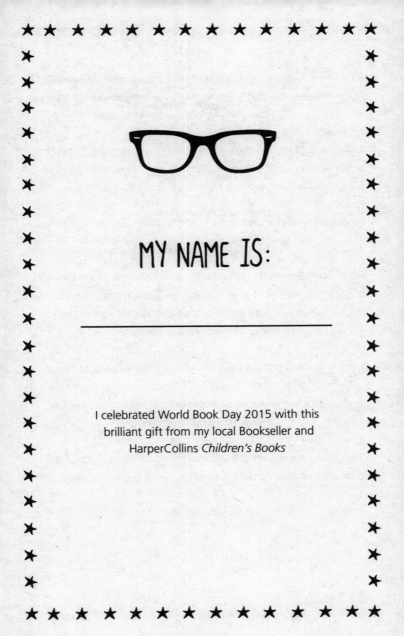

MY NAME IS:

_____

I celebrated World Book Day 2015 with this
brilliant gift from my local Bookseller and
HarperCollins *Children's Books*

Also by **Holly Smale**

Geek Girl

Geek Girl: Model Misfit

Geek Girl: Picture Perfect

Geek Girl: All That Glitters

First published in Great Britain by HarperCollins *Children's Books* 2015
HarperCollins *Children's Books* is a division of HarperCollins *Publishers* Ltd,
HarperCollins *Publishers*
1 London Bridge Street
London SE1 9GF
The HarperCollins *Children's Books* website address is
www.harpercollins.co.uk

1

Geek Girl: Geek Drama
Copyright © Holly Smale 2015

The author asserts the moral right to be identified as the author of this work.

ISBN 978-0-00-811347-6

Printed and bound in England by
Clays Ltd, St Ives plc

89,501
€2·00

MIX
Paper from
responsible sources
FSC C007454

FSC™ is a non-profit international organisation established to promote
the responsible management of the world's forests. Products carrying the
FSC label are independently certified to assure consumers that they come
from forests that are managed to meet the social, economic and
ecological needs of present and future generations,
and other controlled sources.

Find out more about HarperCollins and the environment at
www.harpercollins.co.uk/green

GEEK
DRAMA

HOLLY
SMALE

HarperCollins *Children's Books*

Drama [drah-muh] *noun*

1 A composition in prose or verse presenting in dialogue or pantomime a story involving conflict or contrast of character, especially one intended to be acted on the stage; a play.

2 The branch of literature having such compositions as its subject; dramatic art or representation.

3 Any situation or series of events having vivid, emotional, conflicting or striking interest or results.

4 The quality of being *dramatic*.

ORIGIN 1510s, from Greek *dran,* meaning 'to do, act or perform'.

1

My name is Harriet Manners, and I am an idiot.

I know I'm an idiot because:

1. One half of me is inside a cupboard, and the other is not.
2. I can't move more than two centimetres either backwards or forwards.
3. My feet aren't touching the ground.
4. The shelf I used to climb up to this windowsill collapsed at least forty minutes ago.
5. I keep saying, "Help, help, I'm stuck," even though nobody can hear me.

Clearly my spatial awareness is every bit as terrible as my dance teacher said it was after the Year 10 performance where I accidentally kicked another student in the face during an enthusiastic but badly executed can-can.

I don't fit through this window.

At all.

Frankly, the fact that I even thought I *might* is a cause for serious concern. Recent studies have revealed that domesticated chickens have finely honed sensory capacities and an ability to think, draw inferences, apply logic and plan ahead in more advanced ways than those

11

of a young child.

So, as I've been wedged firmly into the semi-open window of a cleaning cupboard in Infinity Models for forty minutes now, I can't help thinking something, somewhere has gone very badly wrong.

It doesn't say much for your IQ levels when you're a fifteen-year-old girl with less common sense than *poultry.*

2

Anyway, as it looks like I might be here for some time, I might as well tell you how I got here, right?

That's what you want to know.

How a person with over 6,000 days of life experience and an IQ of 135 ended up stuck in a hole like Pooh Bear after a particularly enthusiastic honey session.

And, frankly, I don't blame you.

I'm still kind of trying to work that out myself.

Two hours ago, I was exactly where I was supposed to be: waiting quietly in the reception of Infinity Models.

"Hello," I said as I approached the front desk and tugged at the too-long arms of my stripy jumper. "I'm Harriet Manners. It's nice to meet you. I'm here for a casting."

There was a silence.

"For *Brink* magazine."

Another silence.

"I'm an... erm... model?" I cleared my throat. "A fashion one." In case they thought I meant a small paper aeroplane.

Then I held out my hand.

I've only been in the modelling industry for three months and last time I did this the receptionist assumed I was the work-experience girl. I'd made twelve coffees,

six teas and some headway into cleaning the floor of the photocopying room before anybody had ascertained otherwise.

This time, she didn't even look up.

"Just take a seat, yeah?" she said, waving her hand at the room. I could see from the reflection in the window that she was on a social-networking site.

"Oooh," I said enthusiastically, leaning forwards. "Did you know that particular website contains 140 billion photos, which is four per cent of the number of photos ever taken?"

She looked up and scowled. "*Excuse* me?"

"And you've spelt *depressing* wrong," I said helpfully, pointing at her status update. "*This job is so depressing*. It only has one p. You've got two."

She quickly closed the screen and glared at me.

"I think I'll sit down now," I said, flushing. She was still glaring. "I'll be just over here if you need any more help."

Maybe I shouldn't have convinced Dad to let me do this casting alone after all. It was looking like I'd need armed protection.

I abruptly took a seat in between a beautiful, tanned brunette girl with cropped hair and a blonde with incredibly pale skin and black eyebrows. Then I gripped my hands together tightly so nobody would see they were starting to get clammy.

I hadn't learnt much about fashion, but I knew you had to pretend you belonged there or somebody would immediately realise you didn't and throw you back out again.

So I plastered on my brightest smile.

"Hello," I said. "I'm Harriet Manners. Are you both here to see *Brink* too?"

"Uh-huh." The blonde looked me up and down. "What are you *wearing*?"

I looked down in confusion. Just how literal did she want me to be?

"A striped jumper," I said anxiously. "And a pair of striped leggings." I paused. "And underwear, obviously, and two socks. And green trainers."

"Uh-huh," she said again.

Quick, Harriet. Change the subject.

"Is that you?" I said, pointing at the open folder in the brunette's lap. There was a stunning black and white photo of a very beautiful girl in a bikini, with an enormous cat wrapped around her neck.

She lifted her chin slightly. "Obviously."

"Cats are so interesting, aren't they? Apparently they have a brain the same size as a great white shark's, and jaws with the same strength as a Komodo dragon."

Yup. It's this kind of conversational dynamite that makes not many people want to sit next to me at lunchtime.

The brunette looked at me, and I was saved from my third "uh-huh" by a door swinging abruptly open.

"Baby-baby koala!" my agent, Wilbur, shouted, holding his hands out wide so that the pink sequinned poncho he was wearing made him look like some kind of disco bat. "Come and give me a big cuddle! Not literally, obviously. This is Versace," he said, indicating his outfit, "and it would totally crush my sparkles."

"Hi, Wilbur," I mumbled as he dragged me off my seat

15

and started trying to spin me around in circles as if we were at some kind of shiny country dance.

"Munchkin, I'm so glad you're here. This photographer is just a *desperationist* to see you."

I flushed with surprise. "Really?"

"For *shizzlenizzle*," he said, holding me at arm's length. "They love themselves a good bit of ginger frog now and then. And, oh my holy chicken-unicorns, what are you wearing?"

I grimaced. "It was the first thing that fell out of my wardrobe. Sorry."

"*Genius!* I've always wondered what a human zebra would look like, and now I know!" Wilbur gave me an air-kiss. "We'll be ready for you in four minutes, bunnycakes. Frankly, everyone else might as well go home now. *Brink* are absolutely set on you, my little peach drop. The job is pretty much *yours*."

And then my agent spread his glittery pink wings and disappeared as loudly as he'd arrived.

Slowly, I turned to look at the models sitting behind me.

I read somewhere that ants can survive in a microwave because they are small enough to dodge the rays that would kill them.

Judging from the expressions on these models' faces now, my two options were either to turn into an ant or to spin slowly in circles before finally exploding.

"Umm," I said nervously as the glares intensified. "Have you met Wilbur before?"

"He's our agent too," the blonde model said tightly. "Believe it or not."

"Ah. Right." I coughed and looked desperately at the

receptionist. "Is there… umm… perhaps a bathroom I could use?"

"It's down the stairs, out in the corridor," the receptionist said, pointing with lowered eyelids. "Corridor. Spelt *c-o-r-r-i-d-o-r.*"

I flushed a bit harder.

"Thanks."

Then I disappeared out on to the stairs as quickly as my zebra legs would carry me.

After all, a lot of things can happen in four minutes.

In four minutes, lightning strikes the earth an average of 14,400 times. In four minutes, there are twenty earthquakes and 482,692 pounds of edible food is thrown away in the United States.

Every four minutes, 418 people around the world die.

And, if I stayed in the same place, it was starting to look increasingly likely that I would be one of them.

3

Suffice to say, I locked the bathroom door behind me.

I then spent the next four minutes doing the following:

1. Prodding a painful spot on my cheek.
2. Washing the nervous sweat off my hands.
3. Realising that prodding a spot with sweaty hands was probably part of the problem.
4. Making goldfish faces at myself in the mirror.
5. Drying my hands on toilet paper because scientists have proven that hand dryers actually increase the bacteria levels on your hands by 255 per cent.

Finally, I glanced at my watch, tried to flatten my frizzy hair by smacking it against the sides of my head and then started slowly making my way back out into the hallway.

Where I abruptly stopped.

Both the blonde girl and the brunette were standing in the corridor, leaning against the wall.

"Umm, hello?"

"We've been sent down to the *Brink* casting early," the blonde said, shrugging and pointing at a black door at the bottom of the stairs. "The receptionist wanted to make a private phone call."

I stared at the door in surprise.

"It's down there?" I'd only been to a handful of castings

in my entire life, and they'd all been held in the back room of the agency upstairs. "Really?"

"Awwww, you haven't been modelling very long, have you?" the brunette said, tilting her head sympathetically.

"N-n-no," I admitted, feeling my cheeks get slightly red. *Sugar cookies*. How could they tell?

They both smiled.

"Well, Infinity always put their most important clients downstairs. This is their biggest room, it has the best lighting, and there's a certain… What would you call it…?"

"*Fragrance.*" The blonde picked an invisible bit of fluff off her skinny jeans, then began strutting down the stairs with the brunette following her.

"Yeah. *Fragrance.*"

"Oh." You see? This was exactly the kind of thing I'd know if I hadn't annoyed the receptionist so quickly. "Thanks for letting me know."

I walked down the stairs and stood awkwardly next to them.

"Erm," I said after a few seconds of even more awkward silence. "I'm really sorry about what Wilbur said. Don't worry, I'm not very good at this. As soon as *Brink* meet me they'll change their minds and pick one of you instead."

The models shrugged in unison.

I beamed at them. "So maybe we could start afresh?"

Oh yes, I thought with an excited lurch: *this could be it*. I could make friends with two beautiful models and join their modelling gang. We would become inseparable, and all our fashion adventures henceforth would be conducted as some kind of triumvirate: like in *Harry Potter*, but a fashion version.

I'm freckly and ginger, so I'd be Ron Weasley, obviously.

"You know what?" said the blonde, laughing.

I laughed. This was going *so well already*. We already had our own little in-jokes, even if I didn't really understand them. "What?"

"I reckon this is the perfect place to start *afresh*. You'll be so clean you won't know what to do with yourself."

And as my arms got grabbed and I found myself flung into a cleaning cupboard, all I could think was: a person who believes anything they're told is called a *gobemouche*.

Sounds about right.

4

So that's where I am now.

Not just locked in a cupboard with no working light bulb, no phone reception and the intense smell of an abandoned swimming pool, but halfway through a window.

It became clear after about twenty minutes that I don't like small, confined spaces and I am nowhere near as nimble or as athletic as I'd like to be.

And that it was quite unlikely anybody would be desperately looking for me.

Because that's what happens when you correct other people's spelling: they don't tend to spend much time trying to see you again.

On the upside, I haven't been entirely unproductive. In fact, in the last forty minutes I have managed to:

1. Complete sixteen games of noughts and crosses in the dust on the window ledge.
2. Study a pigeon in the alleyway.
3. Recite the periodic table backwards, forwards and then inside out.
4. Sing my favourite songs from at least seven Disney movies.

389,501

I'm just pondering if the eighth should be *Supercalifragilisticexpialidocious* or *A Whole New World* when I hear the door open behind me.

"Oh, thank sugar cookies," I breathe in relief, wiggling my toes slightly. "I'm so sorry, Wilbur. I'm such a gullible idiot."

Two hands gently grab my waist.

"You know what's ironic?" I say as my jeans belt is unhooked from where it's twisted round the window catch and I'm lowered softly to the ground. "I've never seen anywhere quite as dirty as this place purporting to clean things."

There's a warm laugh, and my toes immediately stop wiggling.

The hottest observed place on earth is Furnace Creek in Death Valley: in 1913 it measured 56.7 degrees Celsius, or 134 degrees Fahrenheit. They might have to recalculate that because right now my cheeks are giving the Californian desert a run for its money.

I spin around slowly and stare into the dark, slanted eyes of the most beautiful boy I have ever seen. His hair is huge and black and curly, his skin is the colour of coffee, his bottom lip is slightly too large and his nose turns up at the end like a ski-slope. The corner of his mouth is twisted up a little, and I happen to know that when he smiles it breaks his whole face in two and the insides of everyone in a ten-mile radius simultaneously.

Of all the people I wanted to see me with my bottom stuck halfway through a window, the only boy I've ever kissed was pretty much at the end of the list.

Him and whoever hands out the Nobel prizes,

you know.

Just in case.

"Umm, hello Nick," I say coolly, sticking my chin in the air as regally as I can. He smells green, even in a cupboard full of bleach.

"Hi Harriet. Were you under the impression that you've recently turned into a cat?"

It's dark in here, but not quite dark enough: I can still see the end of his nose twitching in amusement.

"Of course not." I try to lift my chin a little bit more. "I was just… umm…" *What*? What am I doing in a cupboard? "Keen to see as many elements of the fashion industry as possible. It's important to get a really *rounded* view of modelling. From, you know, different angles."

I clear my throat.

"Uh-huh," he says, except this is nothing like the *uh-huh* the models gave me an hour ago. It's a warm *uh-huh*. An amused *uh-huh*. An *I inexplicably understand what happened without being told and I don't think any less of you for it* uh-huh.

"Umm." I swallow. "What are you doing here?"

He grins and takes a step towards me. "I had to pick up a Versace contract from Wilbur, and he told me you'd gone missing. He's checking under all the tables in the building, and I'm doing all the cupboards."

My cheeks get steadily hotter.

Just because the first time I ever met Nick Hidaka I was hiding under a table doesn't mean I'm *always* under one. I've seen him several times outside of furniture too.

His memory is *very* selective.

We stare each other out for a few seconds.

Clearly the only way to get out of this predicament in style is to stalk out of the cupboard. To stick my nose in the air, be dignified, and charge out in an adult, sophisticated kind of—

A bubble of embarrassed laughter pops out of my mouth.

Nope, that wasn't it, was it?

"I'm a ninny, aren't I?" I say, twisting my mouth and staring at the floor.

"A little bit," Nick laughs in his warm Australian twang.

"I try really hard but I'm not entirely sure I can help it," I admit. "It seems to be inbuilt."

Nick puts a hand under my chin and gently tilts my head back up so I'm looking at him again. "Luckily, I have a soft spot for ninnies. Especially the kind that can recite the periodic table backwards."

And as the boy I like best in the world leans down to kiss me, suddenly a cupboard doesn't seem like the worst place in the world to be stuck in after all.

5

Sadly, we don't get to stay in there.

I pitch for it quite hard. I suggest a cupboard picnic: I'm pretty sure I have a few bits of broken chocolate bar at the bottom of my satchel and, if I rummage hard enough, half a cheese and onion sandwich we can split in two.

Basically anything that will prolong my time in what now magically appear to be incredibly romantic surroundings.

Unfortunately, Nick has other ideas.

"Isn't there somewhere you're supposed to be?"

"The casting?" I poke my head out of the cupboard and frown. The lights of the corridor upstairs have all been turned off. "I think everyone's gone now. It doesn't matter. I wasn't that bothered anyway."

I lean up to kiss him again.

"Nope," Nick laughs, kissing the end of my nose instead. "Not *Brink*. Somewhere else."

Sugar cookies. Why does he always remember everything I say? If I didn't know better, I'd think Nick had my life itinerary bullet pointed and stashed away in his pocket somewhere.

Which is totally the kind of thing I'd do, but I didn't think it was his style.

"Oh," I say airily, waving a hand, "I guess I've missed it by now. Never mind."

Nick lifts an eyebrow. "I'm not sure Nat would see it

like that."

Nat.

I'm suddenly flooded with a wave of shame and guilt so intense I almost fall over. Because I'm going to be honest: if there was another bright side to being stuck in a cupboard, it was that I couldn't be anywhere *else*.

Somewhere even worse.

I look at the floor. "I suppose I *did* promise," I admit in a small voice. "And she is my best friend."

Only friend.

Now is probably not the time to make that clarification.

"Exactly." Nick grins and leans towards me. "It'll be fun. No biggy."

We all know what he means when he says that, which is: exactly the opposite. I try to look cross, which is almost impossible when you're being kissed.

"Next you'll be telling me to break a leg," I mutter grumpily.

Nick laughs and grabs my hand. "Come on, Table Girl. There's a train to your school in fifteen minutes. I'll walk you to the station."

6

Yup: school.

It's 6:30pm on a Saturday evening, and I'm now standing back outside the gates of what should really be a closed building. Usually I'd be delighted to be here out of hours, but right now, frankly, there are other places I'd rather be.

Anywhere, actually.

The winds on Neptune reach at least 2,000 kilometres per hour and are capable of ripping a building to shreds. After a bit of consideration, I'd probably choose to hang out there instead.

"Where have you *been*?" Nat charges towards me like Boudicca on the back of a chariot: perfectly straightened hair flying, perfectly lined eyes narrowed and what I guess is an expensive silver handbag wielded like some kind of boxy shield. "I've been calling for hours and left a billion messages and—" She frowns and looks down. "Harriet, why do you have a ring of dirt around your waist?"

I tug at my stripy jumper. I now look like a grubby human version of Saturn. "I'm so sorry I'm late."

My best friend takes a deep breath and then lets it out with one smooth hand gesture, like a composer about to conduct an orchestra. "It's OK. There's still time."

Sugar cookies. There was still a tiny bit of me hoping I'd managed to totally miss the whole thing.

The horrible, selfish, terrible-friend part, obviously.
Break a leg.

Oooh. That's quite a good idea. If I can just find a few stairs to fall down, I might be able to—

"Don't even think about it," Nat snaps as I start frantically searching the school corridors for some kind of stepped elevation. "I mean it, Harriet. Don't even *think* about thinking about it. You're auditioning for *Hamlet* with me if I have to wheel you up there in a shopping trolley."

Every now and then I wish I didn't have a best friend who knows me inside and out.

Now is definitely one of those times.

"But you don't even *like* Shakespeare, Nat," I point out. I'm going to give it one last shot. "You use *Julius Caesar* to prop up your magnifying mirror."

Nat pulls a face, and I suddenly realise how nervous she is. There's a pink flush on her neck and she's nibbled off all but one varnished nail: her stomach must be full of tiny bits of blue enamel.

Nat sticks her thumb in her mouth and starts attacking the final nail. "This is my last chance, Harriet. If I can't be a model then an actress is the next best thing, right? Maybe I can get some kind of lipstick campaign this way instead."

I flinch.

This is exactly why I agreed to audition with her in the first place. Three months ago, I accidentally stole my best friend's lifelong dream of modelling while on a school trip in Birmingham. The least I can do is support her while she tries to find a different one.

I just wish she'd picked astrophysics. Or gardening.

"Please?" Nat adds in a tiny voice. "I think I might really enjoy it."

She gives me the round-eyed look I've been a sucker for since we were five, and I rally and put my arm around her. "You're going to be amazing, Nat. Let's do it. I mean, what's the worst that can happen?"

Then we open the door to the gym and that question is no longer rhetorical.

Apparently dolphins shed the top layer of their skin every two hours, and there's a chance I may now be turning into one. It feels like every cell on my outer body is falling off far too quickly for a human being.

This can't be happening. It can't be.

But it is.

In the gym hall are two chairs featuring Mr Bott, our English teacher, and our drama teacher, Miss Hammond. On a makeshift stage in the middle is a Year 10 boy, attempting some kind of half-hearted backflip. On the floor is what appears to be nearly half of our entire year group, chatting quietly and playing on their phones: all one hundred and fifty of them.

And right at the front, in the middle of a number of her minions, is the person I thought was least likely to turn up for an extracurricular play audition.

My bully of ten years, my nemesis, my arch-enemy, my foe.

The girl in the world who hates me the most.

Alexa.

7

Seriously.

I've turned up for two auditions in the last four hours. Why couldn't *this* be the one I got locked in a cupboard for?

Nat's face has gone so abruptly white that her blusher is standing out like the two pink spots on a Russian doll.

"I don't understand," she whispers as we slip in and sit quietly on the floor at the back. "Why is everybody here? I thought it would be just the drama keen-beans."

And with one swift chew, the last few shreds of blue nail varnish disappear.

"Apparently, if you take part in the play you don't have to do homework for the entire duration of the rehearsals," a girl in front of us says, over her shoulder. "Like, *any*. Not even maths."

My stomach twists. This is so unfair: I have to do a play *and* miss homework? It's my favourite bit about education: you get to do schoolwork without actually being *at* school.

Then I brighten.

There are approximately eighty girls here and only two female parts in *Hamlet*: if this many people audition, my chances of getting a role are statistically reduced to almost nothing. All I need to do is stay as quiet as I can and maybe they won't even notice I'm—

"Harriet!"

30

I close my eyes momentarily.

"Harriet! Harriet! Harriet Manners!"

Everyone in a fifteen-metre radius stops chatting and spins to look at a cheery figure waving energetically at me. He's wearing orange trousers and a bright blue T-shirt that says:

NEVER TRUST AN ATOM, THEY MAKE UP EVERYTHING

I give a tiny nod and then curl myself up into a ball and try to disappear into myself like a hedgehog.

It doesn't work.

"You're here!" Toby fake-whispers loudly, standing up and starting to pseudo-crouch-step towards me. "I was *certain* you said you'd be here, but then I was worried if maybe that listening device I set up outside your house wasn't working properly and I was going to return to the shop and ask for my money back. But technology prevails! You're actually here!"

Never mind a hedgehog. I've now shrunk to the size of a particularly embarrassed woodlouse.

"Hi Toby," I murmur as my stalker starts charging not very carefully across the people sitting on the floor between us.

"*Ow!*" somebody mutters as he steps on one of their fingers.

"*Oi!*" another person snaps as he kicks their bag a few metres across the room.

"Who invited the geeks?"

Toby continues, totally unabashed. "What part are you going to be auditioning for, Harriet?" he says happily, plonking down next to me. "I think you would make an *excellent* Ophelia, although you might want to rethink because of all the singing. I've stood outside your bathroom window in the morning and it is not one of your many profound talents."

A snigger goes round my immediate vicinity.

There's a long curtain a few metres away: if only I had more defined stomach muscles I might be able to shimmy behind it like a snake.

"Toby," I mutter as my cheeks start getting hot, "I don't think I—"

Toby is waving a piece of paper. "I've narrowed down your possible audition speeches to Kate from *The Taming of the Shrew*, and Lady Macbeth. How good are you at cleaning up blood?"

Half the room is now nudging each other and giggling. My cheeks get a bit hotter as I glance nervously at Alexa at the front. She's staring blankly at the boy on stage, who is now inexplicably doing some kind of juggling act. "Toby…"

"Or the eponymous Juliet."

"Toby…"

"Or Desdemona from *Othello*. The bit where she dies." He pauses. "Except she sings too. Maybe scrap that one."

Fifteen more people turn to giggle.

"Or—"

And – just like that – my entire head explodes. "TOBY, PLEASE, FOR THE LOVE OF SUGAR COOKIES. GO AWAY."

Then there's an abrupt silence while the entire room spins to look at us.

Yeah. I don't think that helped much.

"*Harriet Manners.*"

Mr Bott is standing at the front of the room with his arms folded and his face creased up like a damp pair of socks.

Oh no. Oh no oh no oh – "Yes?"

"Stand up please."

I cautiously uncurl myself from the floor and somehow get to my feet. My entire face is now pulsing red like the pause button on our washing machine at home.

Mr Bott's face gets just a little sock-ier.

"From what I recall, Harriet, this is not the first time you have chosen to disrupt others by shouting. After your last little display, I'm surprised you haven't learnt your lesson."

Last term, I accidentally yelled at Toby in the middle of an English class, which led to getting in trouble with Mr Bott, which led to accidentally upsetting Alexa, which led to her forcing everyone to put their hands up to say they hated me.

I'm quite surprised I didn't learn my lesson too.

Maybe they need to do a class on that instead.

"I'm sorry," I say in a small voice.

Mr Bott raises his eyebrows. "As you're obviously so *eager* to be a pivotal part of this production, why don't you come up next?"

I look at the stage.

Then at the staring, silent crowd around me. Then at Alexa, who has spun round and narrowed her eyes at me. Then at Toby, who infuriatingly beams and puts both thumbs in the air.

Finally, I look at Nat.

"Please?" she whispers. "I don't want to do it on my own."

I think of what happened last time I was on a stage: I accidentally knocked another model to the floor and ruined an entire fashion show.

Then I think of where I've been today: at a modelling-agency casting for *Brink* magazine (or attempting to be, anyway). I think of how much my best friend of a decade would have given to be there instead.

Then I swallow and grab the piece of paper out of Toby's hand.

"All right," I say as loudly as I can. "I'll do it."

And I make my way up on to the stage.

8

There's a small fresh-water animal called a *hydra* that lives in ponds, lakes and streams.

The hydra can be torn completely into pieces, and it'll still be OK. The bits of it will, cell by cell, creep and crawl towards each other and reassemble, forming a hydra again.

There's just one condition: some of the brain cells have to remain unharmed throughout. The secret to the hydra's survival is keeping its head.

Sadly, I am not a hydra.

As soon as I stand on the stage, my brain disintegrates. I know Juliet's speech by heart – sometimes I recite it in the bath, just for fun – but I'm desperately scanning the script clutched in my sweaty hands because now I can't remember a single word.

Every time I look at Nat, I know I have to try as hard as I can to get a part in the play. Every time I think about performing in front of the entire school, I know I have to try as hard as I can *not* to.

And every time I look at Alexa, sitting two metres away with a smug smile, all I want to do is run behind a curtain or down a hole in the floorboards somewhere.

Plus there's my innate lack of acting talent to contend with. I love Shakespeare, but I appreciate it *academically*. My artistic abilities are, as ever, non-existent.

So I just have to get this over with as fast as possible before I'm ripped apart.

Sugar cookies. Sugar cookies sugar cookies sugar c—

"O Romeo, *Romeo!*" I blurt nervously, clutching hard at my chest as if I'm having a small coronary. "Wherefore art thou... umm..." I hold the paper in front of my face. "Sorry, I've lost my place."

"She speaks!" Toby says from the side of the room where he's edged closer. "Oh, speak again, bright angel!"

The whole room starts sniggering again.

Alexa raises her eyebrows and her smile gets a little cattier.

"Err..." I briefly consider curling up into a ball and rolling off the stage, and then glance at Nat and decide against it. "Deny thy father and refuse thy name; Or, if thou wilt not..."

Alexa rolls her eyes and yawns elaborately.

"...I'll no longer be a Montague. No, sorry, a Capulet. I'm a Capulet."

"Shall I hear more, or shall I speak at this?"

"I think you should probably be quiet, Toby," Miss Hammond says firmly. "Or you'll be asked to leave the room."

"But Harriet is the sun," Toby objects.

"That's as maybe, but I suggest you enjoy her silently."

Toby pulls a pretend zip across his mouth and winks at me from the corner of the stage. I'm going to kill him when I get out of here, and not a single jury in the country will convict me, due to the reasonable circumstances.

I take a deep breath.

Keep your head, Harriet.

"Tisbutthynamethatismyenemythouartthyselfthough notaMontaguewhatsMontagueitisnorhandnorfootnor armnorfacenoranyotherpartbelongingtoamanobesomeother namewhatsinanamethatwhichwecallarosebyanyoth ernamewouldsmellassweetsoromeowouldwerehe notromeocalledretainthatdearperfection—"

"OK," Mr Bott says, holding up his hand. "I think that will do. Thank you, Harriet. That was… illuminating."

Alexa starts a slow, sarcastic clap.

"And that will do too, Alexa Roberts," Mr Bott adds sharply.

"*What*, sir?" Alexa says innocently. "I was simply showing my enthusiasm for Harriet's profound and inspiring performance."

"I find that hard to believe," my English teacher says fairly. "So let's move on as fast as possible, shall we? Next."

9

The next hour is like watching some kind of terribly amateur circus.

I slink to my position with Nat at the back of the hall and sit as quietly as I can while my cheeks return to their normal colour.

Luckily, there's plenty to distract me on stage.

There are people doing cartwheels, people singing, people dancing, people pretending to 'breathe fire' with a lighter and a small aerosol (they get a detention). Somebody even brought their dog with them, except instead of jumping through a hoop it sits down on the stage and farts resplendently.

All of which would be a lot less surprising if there wasn't a sign on the door saying:

THIS IS NOT ITV

Finally it's Nat's turn. She stands up and smooths her hair down and I can feel myself starting to get genuinely excited.

Maybe she's going to be good.

No: maybe she's going to be *great*. Maybe this is the amazing future my best friend is destined for, and this will be the moment that changes everything. In ten years' time I'll be lying under a parasol by her Hollywood pool,

applying SPF 50, because I don't really have skin that tolerates Californian weather.

"Good luck," I whisper as she squeezes my hand tightly.

And then – with great poise – Nat walks slowly on to the stage and stands very still for a few seconds, looking at us calmly.

I stare at her in astonishment.

All anxiety, all jitteriness, every bit of nerves has magically disappeared. In their place is total composure and dignity. *Tranquility*. A deep and unshakeable aura of confidence and self-belief.

A serenity falls over the room and we are all utterly under her spell. I have never been so proud in my entire life.

Then Nat opens her mouth.

"*Now*," she says stiffly, running to one side of the stage and holding one hand to her forehead as if she's got a debilitating fever, "is the *winter* of our *discontent*. *Parting* is *such* sweet sorrow I shall say *goodnight* till it be *morrow*." She runs to the other side of the stage. "*Rough* winds do *shake* the darling *buds* of May, and is *this* a dagger I see before me?"

She collapses on to the floor and starts pretend-wailing into her hands. "*Shall* I compare *thee* to a summer's day?" She stares at the ceiling and wrings her hands. "If *music* be the *food* of *love* play *on*…"

I watch with increasing alarm as my best friend commences to fling herself around, punch the air, jump, hop, scream and flounce across the stage. One second she's Macbeth, the next she's Othello. Without a pause she's rolling around on her back, wailing for Cordelia, and then – seamlessly – she's Puck, then Beatrice, then Desdemona.

Finally – when she's exhausted what feels like a disco-mash-up of the entire Shakespearean canon – Nat ends by crashing to her knees and doing what appears to be jazz-hands.

Maybe we should have gone over her audition strategy a little more closely before we got here.

Or – you know. At all.

"So am I in?" Nat finally asks eagerly, looking up as Mr Bott puts his head in his hands. "Can I be Hamlet?"

Miss Hammond glances at Mr Bott, and together they slowly stand up. "And that wraps up the auditions," they say in unison. "Thanks for coming, everyone."

"Well," I hear Mr Bott mutter as they stalk quickly past on their way out of the hall, "it's good to see that the last few years of my life have clearly been wasted."

The door slams behind them.

Nat looks at me over the top of the assembled crowd and I smile a bit harder. There are forty-three muscles in the human face, and I now have such an unnatural expression I'm worried I may have strained a few of them.

I pinch my cheek experimentally.

"Oh, that I were a glove upon that hand, that I might touch that cheek!" a voice says from behind me. "Can you see what I'm doing, Harriet? I'm being Romeo for you."

I spin round crossly. "Why are you here, Toby? You didn't even *audition*."

40

"I'm not here to audition, Harriet," he says in surprise. "Sometimes I really don't think you understand the concept of stalking."

I sigh in frustration. "Now would be quite a good time to leave me alone, Toby," I say as politely as I can. "Seriously. Please."

"Gotcha," he says happily. "Disappearing."

And he blithely scarpers out of the room with his undone shoelaces trailing behind him.

I grit my teeth and start walking as fast as I can towards the exit door, away from the madding crowds. I need some peace and quiet to reassemble again like a hydra, and I need it quickly.

Except I can't have it.

As I turn to open the door to the outside world, a foot appears in front of me and jams it shut.

"Did you forget something, Manners?"

And there, physically blocking my path with my satchel in her arms, is Alexa.

10

So.

I have this theory that being a geek is a bit like being a polar bear in the middle of the rainforest.

You don't fit in, and you never will.

And it doesn't matter how many trees you try to hide behind, or how many times you get on your belly and crawl through the undergrowth, or how fervently you put your hand over your nose to try and camouflage yourself, you can't hide.

Trust me. I've tried.

Nat, on the other hand, is a tiger.

We've been best friends for ten years, and she has never once apologised for being who she is or tried to change. She simply prowls through the chaos in her perfect make-up and her five-inch heels, growling at anyone who gets in the way.

Which means they never do, because nobody messes with a tiger.

But, in between all the flying squirrels and bright green frogs and monkeys and baboons, Alexa goes unnoticed until it is too late. She slips in quietly, and you never know when it's going to be or where she's going to come from.

Just what she's going to do.

She'll set her sights on you, hone in on the soft parts – the bits you can't protect – and then she'll insert her

42

poison. She'll irritate and prod and pick so that when the time comes it's easier for her to digest you completely.

Then she'll leave, taking a tiny piece of you with her.

In short: of all the animals in the world, my bully is by far the most dangerous. She contributes the least, she's impossible to get rid of, and she spreads damage wherever she goes.

Alexa is the mosquito.

=

Continuing our rainforest theme, there's a frog that lives in Central Africa called the *Trichobatrachus Robustus*. In order to protect itself, it will painfully break its own bones until they pierce out of its toe pads like claws.

Like an amphibian version of Wolverine.

As I stare at Alexa's deceptively pretty face, I can totally see where the frog's coming from. I'm kind of tempted to break my own knuckles and give it a go.

"That's my satchel," I say in surprise, looking at it.

I must have left it on the floor in my urgency to get out of the room, like a total idiot.

"Well, obviously," she says, pointing at the red letters spelling GEEK etched once more proudly and freshly on the front in red pen. My spirits sink: they took absolutely ages to scrub off last time. "I picked it up for you, Harriet. Aren't you going to say thank you?"

Harriet? She's called me a lot of names before, but never the one I've actually been legally registered with.

"Umm." I swallow reluctantly. *Thanks for vandalising my property yet again.* "Mmm."

"That's OK. You know, I'm just so excited about this play," she continues, smiling and leaning against the door slightly with my satchel still in her hands. "It's a really *unique* opportunity."

What?

I spent the entire hour with my hands clenched together, waiting for Alexa to get up on stage, but she didn't. I even checked with a few people in our immediate vicinity, and apparently she didn't audition before we got there, either. I'd assumed she was just there to intimidate other people.

Or, more specifically: me.

"You're excited about the prospect of extra time at school?" I say doubtfully.

"Absolutely," she beams at me. "I love a good bit of drama. It's so *cathartic*, isn't it?"

"Um, traditionally, yes."

"So fingers crossed we both get parts, hey?" Alexa says as she hands me my newly destroyed satchel and opens the door politely.

I look anxiously at my satchel, and then at the door. Is she going to shut me in it like a Venus flytrap? Is my satchel going to explode like a leather, pencil-filled hand-grenade?

"OK." Then I cautiously take a few steps forward.

Nothing happens.

"See you soon, Harriet Manners," Alexa smiles sweetly as I manage to step outside. "Ooh." She pauses. "What hotel do mice stay at?"

I blink. "Excuse me?"

"It's just a *joke*, Harriet," she says, blowing me a kiss. "Let me know when you work out the punchline."

And then she closes the hall door softly behind me.

12

People can change, you know.

I firmly believe that humans can surprise you with unexpected kindness, previously untapped empathy and depths of niceness and compassion you never knew they had.

But Alexa is unlikely to be one of them.

She's definitely got something unpleasant up her sleeve. I just don't know what it is yet.

With limited enthusiasm, I sit on the wall on the other side of the road from the school gates while I tug the cells of my scattered head back together and try to change the word GEEK now scrawled on my bag to CREEK with the same shade of red pen.

I can pretend it's a reference to my interest in the Antietam Creek in Pennsylvania, which was a key focal point of the Battle of Antietam during the American Civil War.

That'll work.

Then I see Nat approaching from a distance, and a ridiculous mental rerun of the last two hours starts tumbling through my head.

The wailing. The hand gestures. The rolling around on the floor. The stammering. Toby's interruptions.

Between us, possibly two of the worst performances

of Shakespeare ever witnessed, and that includes the guy who vomited on himself halfway through last year's *Othello*.

By the time Nat actually reaches me, I'm giggling so hard I keep making little snorty noises like one of those miniature pigs celebrities keep in their handbags.

"Oh my goodness," I say as she sits on the wall next to me. *Snort.* "Nat, that was…" *Snort snort.* "It was… haha… Just so…" *Snort.*

"*Amazing*, right?"

I abruptly stop oinking. "Huh?"

Nat drops her handbag down next to her, eyes glittering and cheeks bright pink. "This is it, Harriet. I've found my natural calling. It's meant to be."

My eyes open wide.

"I mean, obviously I need a bit of *polishing* here and there," Nat continues, pulling her hair into a ponytail. "I'm not classically trained yet. But I really became someone else on stage, didn't I? I *transformed*. It was…" She looks into the sky with a rapt expression. "*Magic*."

I stare at my best friend.

Admittedly it looked like there was *some* kind of voodoo at work, but it felt slightly on the darker end of the enchantment scale.

"You were…" I start carefully. "Something else."

Nat bites her lip proudly and goes a little pinker. "I know, right? There was a moment where I thought Miss Hammond was actually going to cry."

"That's quite possible," I say honestly.

Then I look carefully at Nat. She's lit up from the inside, like one of those environmentally damaging lanterns people let off at New Year. "Umm, Nat?"

"Mmm?" she says as we start walking home, trailing her handbag dreamily behind her.

"What... erm... *part* were you playing, exactly?"

"Don't know." Nat beams triumphantly. "I found the speech on the internet last night. It must have been Shakespeare's most famous play though. I'd actually heard almost all the lines already."

"Ah." This is exactly why we are given set, governmentally approved texts at school. "Of course."

"The cast list goes up on Monday," Nat says, holding her hands together and spinning around. "And then... my life's about to change forever. I can *feel* it. There'll be an agent in the crowd, and they'll spot me and it'll be *just* like a Richard Curtis film. Just wait and see."

She glances at me and her grin falters a bit.

"You were great as well," she lies loyally. "Don't worry, Harriet. They'll give you a good role too, I'm sure of it."

"That's really not what I'm worried about."

Nat puts her arm through mine. "Thanks for coming with me. You're the best friend in the world, you know that?"

My insides *ping* with guilt.

"Mmmm," I say, pulling at the sleeves of my jumper. "So... see you on Monday morning?"

"Definitely," Nat says, already starting to focus on a chimney in the distance. "I'm going to start getting ready for my big day. I should probably wear all black and a beret so I look suitably arty for my new career."

"Mmm," I say again.

And then I peck her on the cheek and start trotting

back to my house as fast as I possibly can.

There are less than forty-eight hours before that cast list goes up, and I need to work out exactly what to do before Nat sees it.

Thanks partly to me, she's already had one dream destroyed in the last three months.

There is absolutely no way I'm letting it happen again.

13

Home.

At the end of a hard day, it's really nice to return to a serene, calming, tidy place: one that makes you feel like the world makes sense.

One day, I'm going to work out exactly where that is.

"Annabel?" I say as I push open the front door and drop my satchel in the hallway. "Dad? Are you here?"

I'm not sure why I'm asking.

My stepmother, Annabel, is four months' pregnant with my brand new sibling, so is rarely out in the evenings, and Dad is still unemployed. After he loudly told his biggest client to get lost in the reception of the advertising agency he worked at, nobody has given him an interview.

It's a small industry, Dad says, and apparently they're quite happy with it being that little bit smaller.

"No," I hear Annabel say calmly through the doors of the kitchen. "Absolutely not."

"*No*? Is that your final answer?"

"That is my final answer, Richard. *Hercules* is not a responsible name to give a baby."

"I don't see why not. It worked out quite well for Hercules, didn't it? He could lift wheelbarrows before he was out of nappies."

"He was the son of Zeus, Richard. What if our baby isn't half mortal, half god?"

There's a pause.

"Well, of course it will be," Dad says indignantly. "It's genetically related to me, isn't it?"

I roll my eyes and walk into the kitchen.

My father is in his multicoloured, stripy dressing gown – the one that makes him look like he's the star in a West End show – and my stepmother is in a plain black suit, now bulging at quite a few different seams.

Annabel's a barrister, and she loves that suit so much I'm pretty sure she sleeps in it.

"Oh, look," Dad says as I take a seat next to them and pick out a chocolate biscuit from the multi-pack on the table. "We've got a teenager. Did you know that?"

"I knew I'd put one somewhere," Annabel says serenely, spreading green pesto on a KitKat. "I thought she might have fallen down the crack in the sofa or got wedged behind the curtains."

I stick my tongue out at them.

"Haha," I say, cramming a biscuit in my mouth. "You're both hilarious."

Annabel smiles at me. "You're home late, sweetheart. We were starting to worry."

"I wasn't," Dad says, ruffling my hair fondly. "I'd already started working out how to turn her bedroom into a yoga studio and impromptu Batman dungeon."

Annabel laughs and leans over to kiss him.

My parents have been married for eleven years and yet they still seem to quite like each other. It's very uncomfortable on Sport's Day. Nobody else has parents that fist-bump every time the whistle blows.

"So what did you do today? How was the casting?

And the audition?" Annabel asks. "Update us on the adventures of being a modern-day teenager."

I think about the answer to that question.

What did I do today?

Annoyed a receptionist and two models, got locked in a cleaning cupboard, stuck in a window, kissed one boy and shouted at another, was told off by a teacher, humiliated myself on stage and discovered my best friend is a terrible, terrible actress.

Oh, and had my accessories vandalised. Again.

"Fine. I learnt that there is a cult in Malaysia that worships a giant teapot."

It seemed like the best overall response.

They both nod in approval.

"That sounds like my kind of cult," Dad agrees. "Exactly how big is it? I mean, could you get inside it, or is it just big enough for, like, five cups of tea at once? Normal teapots are far too small, if you ask me."

"If you want dinner," Annabel says, lifting her eyebrows at Dad and patting me on the arm, "there's some toast over there and some ice-cream in the freezer you can spread on it if you want."

Seriously. I love my stepmother, but by the time this baby comes I'm going to have died of malnutrition.

I grab what remains of the multi-pack instead.

"I'll just finish these off upstairs," I say. "There's something more important I have to do first."

14

I spend the rest of the weekend eating biscuits, trawling the internet and making a list.

Here are some interesting alternative career options I find for Nat:

1. Water Slide Tester
2. Snake Milker
3. Teddy Bear Repair Technician
4. Fountain Pen Doctor
5. Pet Food Tester

None of which is likely to make my best friend want to drop her stage and screen ambitions.

Snakes don't even have milk, for starters.

By the time Monday morning comes round, I've amassed a considerable range of different job interests, from graphic design to history of art to agriculture. There aren't that many farms in our local area, but you never know what might pique Nat's interest.

Cows can walk up a flight of stairs, but not back down again… she might find that fascinating.

Unfortunately, I don't even get a chance to convince her of any of them, because at 7am I get the following text:

Going into school now to wait outside the drama department for The List. This is just like Christmas morning! Nat xoxo

I stare at the text in dismay, and then pull my uniform on as quickly as I can.

Sugar cookies.

It looks like I might have to implement Plan B sooner than I thought.

The peregrine falcon is the fastest animal on earth, and in an emergency it can dive to the ground at speeds of up to 322 kilometres per hour.

Unfortunately, I can't move anywhere near that fast.

Dad's left the vacuum cleaner in the hallway and as I rush downstairs – keen to speed to Nat's side – I trip over it, ripping a hole in my tights. Then I have to detangle myself, go change my tights and unsuccessfully attempt to avoid a conversation with Annabel about why I never, ever do any vacuuming, even though I make the majority of the mess.

Then my stepmother wants to talk to me about a documentary she's recorded on dolphins.

Then the baby starts kicking, and I spend another ten minutes telling her that at seventeen weeks it is now covered in a layer of thick, downy hair called *lanugo*, so it probably looks like a little werewolf.

When I finally open the front door, Toby springs out from behind the hedge and starts telling me that 8,000 years ago Britain had so many trees that a squirrel could cross the country without ever touching the ground.

I can't help myself from getting into a huge environmental debate about deforestation.

And squirrels.

By the time I finally get to school, it's 9am and I'm late for registration. Nat is already sitting in the seat next to mine, sucking on a strand of her long hair.

I slip in anxiously next to her as our form teacher, Mrs Hart, pauses taking the register and stares at me with an unimpressed expression.

"Any news?" I whisper as I open my satchel and pull out my school diary.

Mrs Hart glares at me, then pointedly continues.

Nat shakes her head. "Apparently they haven't decided yet." Her fingernails are bright tangerine today, but the right index finger is already blank. "I can't stand the suspense, Harriet. I just can't."

I relax slightly. That means there's still time to do something.

Then Nat sniffs and leans towards me.

"Umm," she adds under her breath, "awkward question, but did you skip your shower this morning?"

"What are you talking about?" I surreptitiously lean down and sniff my armpits. "Of course not. It takes two gallons of water to brush your teeth, seven gallons to flush a toilet and 25 to 75 to have a shower. I assure you I have used *all* of them today."

"I believe you," Nat says, frowning. "Weird."

Mrs Hart continues with the register, then pauses and looks up with her nose wrinkled.

"Has somebody dragged something unpleasant in with them?"

The whole class is starting to sit up straight and sniff the air like a mob of meerkats. The smell is getting stronger and stronger: even I can smell it now.

Sour, mouldy, sweaty. Utterly disgusting.

"Ew," Megan says, pulling the sleeve of her school jumper across her nose. "That's horrible."

"I think I'm going to be sick," Sophie states angrily. "Like, actually vomit."

"Miss," one of the boys in the back row calls out optimistically, "I don't think it's fair to work under these conditions. Can we go home?"

"All right," Mrs Hart says tiredly. "There's no need to overreact. Let's just work out where it's coming from, shall we? Everybody check the bottom of their shoes."

Sixty shoes suddenly get shoved on top of the desks while everybody makes a big demonstration of the fact that the rapidly deteriorating smell has nothing to do with them.

Then Mrs Hart gets up and starts walking slowly round the class, inhaling. We all watch her with our breaths held in anticipation (and because it's now really quite unpleasant to breathe).

She circles up and down the rows, back and forth, with her nose twitching like it's attached to an invisible string.

Then she approaches us.

"It's here," she says triumphantly and stops directly in front of me.

Apparently lobsters store bright red pigment in their skins that only becomes visible when heat destroys the other colours.

My cheeks obviously contain precisely the same

molecule.

"I don't smell!" I blurt out before I can stop myself. "It's not me!"

A snigger goes round the classroom.

"She who smelt it dealt it," somebody says from the back, even though that makes no logical sense because I wasn't the one to first bring it up.

"Harriet Manners *stinks*," somebody else shouts. "Like, gross."

"Ewwww, geeks are disgusting."

"Mrs Hart, we shouldn't be forced to take a lesson with somebody who can't clean themselves properly. We're at an educational disadvantage."

My cheeks get a little redder. "I clean myself properly," I say, sitting up as straight as I can. "I've been doing it for years!"

Then I mentally run through every product I've used this morning. Mint toothpaste, chocolate shower-gel, honey shampoo. OK, I might smell like a Christmas stocking, but that's not a bad thing, is it?

"Excuse me, but Harriet Manners doesn't reek," Toby says indignantly from the front desk. "She is beyond such base body functions."

"I'm not saying *you* smell, Harriet," Mrs Hart says patiently as I start frantically looking for a window to jump out of. "I'm only saying the smell is coming from here. Maybe you accidentally stepped in something."

"Or maybe geeks are just rancid," somebody else offers helpfully.

"I'm *not*," I say as my cheeks flame and the bell finally rings. Everyone in the class abruptly loses interest and starts packing their bags. Thank goodness for the ritual of punctual school scheduling.

They file out, one by one, and then – at the very last minute – I see it: Alexa's face, shining with the light of a million smug fireflies.

My satchel. *What hotel do mice stay at?*

The Stilton.

Alexa's so-called joke.

I quickly dig through to the bottom of my satchel, and there it is: a mound of soft, rotting blue cheese. Covered in mould, releasing slightly yellow juices and absolutely stinking.

I pull out the rancid cheese and hold it up.

"Well," Mrs Hart says flatly as she starts packing up her files, "please dispose of that *outside* of my classroom immediately." She walks towards the door. "I have to say, Harriet, that's a *very* strange thing to bring to school with you."

And before I can defend myself, she's followed the rest of the class out of the room.

Leaving me, bright red and stinking of cheese, behind her.

15

So, here are some interesting cheese facts:

1. Cheese has existed for more than 12,000 years, which is longer than recorded history.
2. The world's most expensive cheese is called 'pule', and is made from donkeys' milk.
3. They've created a cheese out of the bacteria found on a human bellybutton and foot.
4. And from the tears of artists and writers.
5. Stilton is almost impossible to clean out of a satchel.

The rest of the morning is spent frantically scrubbing out my bag with bits of wet tissue and a sponge from the art department, to no avail. I still smell like the boys' changing rooms.

Penicillin may have saved an estimated 200 million lives since it was discovered, but its presence in blue cheese has certainly not helped mine much.

I have literally never been less popular.

Eventually I admit defeat, ask the caretaker for a black bin-liner and put my satchel inside that instead. Then I cram my stationery and books into a supermarket carrier bag and run as fast as I can to the drama department.

Maybe it's not too late. Maybe I can still convince them not to crush Nat's ego and dreams and—

"Miss Hammond?"

She's walking down the corridor, necklaces swaying from side to side, rings all the way up to her knuckles. The school has a strict 'no jewellery' policy, and from the looks of it everything that gets confiscated gets given directly to the drama teacher.

"Yes, Harriet?" She glances up momentarily from her clipboard.

I don't want to know how she remembers my name, but it might be from when I managed to fall off the stage while playing a rock in *The Wizard of Oz*.

"Please may I talk to you?" I say urgently, dumping my smelly black bin-liner on the floor. "It's very important."

Miss Hammond nods patiently and I clear my throat. With all the cheese-drama, I haven't had a chance to fully work out my strategy yet. All I know is it needs to be convincing, I need to do it now, and it needs to work fast.

"Did you know," I say, holding my hands together tightly, "that Thomas Edison made 1,000 unsuccessful attempts before he invented the lightbulb?"

Miss Hammond frowns. "Is that so?"

"Yes." I squeeze my hands together a little harder. "And Walt Disney was fired by a newspaper editor for lacking imagination."

"Harriet…"

"And Colonel Sanders had his chicken recipe rejected 1,009 times because nobody liked it. Sony's first ever product was a rice cooker that burnt all the rice…"

"Harriet…"

"Stephen King had *Carrie* rejected thirty times, and Beethoven was completely deaf and apparently rubbish at

60

playing the violin. And don't get me started on J.K. Rowling because the amount of people who didn't believe in her defies bel—"

Miss Hammond puts her hand on my shoulder and all her bracelets start jingling. "*Harriet*. What exactly is it you're trying to say?"

Huh. I thought that was pretty obvious. This is clearly the reason why our drama teacher doesn't work in a law firm. Annabel would have understood historical precedence immediately.

"Please give Natalie Grey a part in *Hamlet*, Miss Hammond. Please. Don't write her off already. She just needs another chance, that's all."

Miss Hammond looks at me for a few seconds and then smiles amiably. "Harriet, the list is already up. I stuck it on the wall five minutes ago."

"But—"

"It's all decided. The dramatic die has been cast, so to speak. Ha. Hahaha."

"*Harriet!*" an urgent voice shouts from round the corner. "*Harriet!* Where are you?"

Miss Hammond beams at me and then spins on her heel and wanders back into her classroom, clinking like the ghost of Marley in *A Christmas Carol*.

I turn just in time to see Nat, charging towards me with a white face and a bright pink piece of paper held high in her hand.

My stomach drops.

"Oh, Nat," I say as she reaches me and wraps me in a tight hug. "I'm so sor—"

"I'm *in!*" she squeaks into my shoulder. "I knew it,

Harriet! I'm going to be a *star!*"

The paper is thrust into my hands and I blink at it a few times over her back, trying to make sense of what's written there.

But I can't.

Because I know *Hamlet*, and it simply doesn't make sense at all.

16

<u>Year 11 Production of Hamlet</u>

Prince Hamlet - Christopher Bell
Ghost of Hamlet's Father - Noah Jackson
King Claudius - Ben Wilson
Queen Gertrude - Kira Macinko
Ophelia - Raya Patel

I read the top of the list three times, just in case I've somehow abruptly lost all my literacy skills.

It still looks the same.

The only two female roles in *Hamlet* have gone to Raya – easily the prettiest girl in our year, with eyelashes like a beautiful deer – and Kira, the girl whose audition piece consisted of the most terrifying Desdemona I'd ever seen. She looked like she could easily beat Othello up and was seriously considering it.

I look back in confusion at Nat, still glowing.

"But—"

"*See?*" she says, pointing at the bottom. Underneath Horatio and Polonius and Laertes, it says:

Yorick - Natalie Grey

"Uh," I manage.

"Isn't it *amazing*?" Nat says happily, kissing the paper that she must have torn off the wall in excitement. "Yorick is really important, Harriet. 'Alas, poor Yorick'. It's, like, the most famous line. I'm Alas Poor Yorick!"

I blink a few times and then scan the paper again.

Just above Nat's name, it says:

Rosenstern - Harriet Manners

"*Rosenstern?*" I echo blankly. "But there *isn't* a Rosenstern. There's a Rosencrantz and a Guildenstern. They're two separate people."

"Yes," Miss Hammond says, emerging into the corridor once more with half a sandwich in her hand. "But they are virtually indistinguishable, so I decided to merge them for efficiency."

Merge them for efficiency? What's next – Roliet? Prosperello?

"And they're *boys*," I object fiercely.

"Shakespeare was only legally allowed to use men to act in his plays for every part," she observes, firmly stuffing the rest of the sandwich in her mouth. "I felt it was about time we redressed the feminist balance. Mia will be playing Horatio."

Great. I don't even want to be in the play and I've essentially been cast as the Tweedle-Dum and Tweedle-Dee of the sixteenth century.

"We corrected a false rumour going round that people would be exempt from homework during rehearsals," Miss Hammond adds nonchalantly. "Bizarrely, quite a few people dropped out this morning."

Suddenly the list is starting to make a little bit more sense.

Then I look at the bottom of the list and my entire stomach flips over.

Light and sound technician - Alexa Roberts

Light. And. Sound. Technician.

Are they *kidding*?

What is *wrong* with teachers? They might as well give Alexa the keys to the kingdom and be done with it. She'll be able to pull all the strings from behind the curtains, like the crazed, power-hungry Wizard of Oz.

Except with expensive blonde highlights and a more brutal disposition.

This is a *disaster*.

"Quick, Harriet," Nat says, dragging me to the side and folding up the cast list tightly. "I never listen in English. What's *Hamlet* about again?"

I swallow. Finally, this is something I can actually help Nat with.

"The King of Denmark has just died," I say, trying to avoid her eyes. "The King's ghost tells his son, Prince Hamlet, that he was murdered by his brother, Claudius, so that he could take the crown and marry Hamlet's mother, Queen Gertrude. Hamlet swears to seek revenge—"

"*Oooh*," Nat breathes. "Exciting."

I nod. "But in the meantime Hamlet dumps his girlfriend, Ophelia, and accidentally kills her father, so she goes totally bonkers and drowns herself."

"*No*," Nat says with round eyes. "What a pig!"

I smile. I've been trying to tell Nat that Shakespeare was the sixteenth century equivalent of a melodramatic TV drama, and that she'd love it as much as I do if she gave it a chance, for years.

"So then Ophelia's brother, Laertes, wants to kill Hamlet for killing his dad and sister, so it all leads up to this big fight where Hamlet poisons Laertes and Claudius poisons Gertrude and Hamlet poisons Claudius and Laertes poisons Hamlet. Basically everyone dies."

Nat looks pretty impressed. "Dark," she says. "What happens to Rosencrantz and Guildenstern?"

"They die."

"And Yorick?" Nat says, taking a deep breath. "Does he die, Harriet? Tell me he dies. I spent all last night working on my death rattle, just in case."

I take a deep breath and finally manage to make eye contact with my best friend.

"Yes," I say as gently as I can. "Yorick dies too."

Which is kind of true.

Because Yorick is a skull. He has no lines, no songs and no costume.

And he's dead the whole way through.

17

I want to tell Nat the truth, but there's no chance. Between classes and homework and extra-homework (me) and 'Yorick preparations' (Nat) I barely see her for the next forty-eight hours.

It's not the kind of news I wanted to break to her via text, and rehearsals start in earnest straight after school on Wednesday.

Mr Bott and Miss Hammond have decided that, instead of a full length, four-hour version of *Hamlet,* it's probably wiser if they reduce it to twenty minutes and book end it with dances from Year 8 and 9.

"For *impact,*" Miss Hammond says, dramatically flinging her arms out so her floral sleeve ruffles go crazy. "You know, make it really short and punchy. Really *grab* the audience and leave a lasting impression."

"And also you lot aren't very good at learning lines," Mr Bott says considerably less dramatically. "So the less time you spend on stage the better."

Miss Hammond scowls at him.

"*Anyway,*" she says brightly, turning to us and clapping her hands together, "the headmaster has decided he would like our performance to be part of the Open Evening for new potential sixth formers, so we have just a couple of weeks to polish it up. We can do it, guys!"

She gaily starts distributing wads of pink paper. I think

she's under the impression that if the play is baby pink, people are going to get more excited about it.

We all stare at each other.

I've never seen a more unlikely group of budding actors. There are just thirteen of us, thanks to what Miss Hammond is calling *Dramatic Efficiency Blending*. Mia is somehow playing Horatio *and* the priest, Noah is playing both the ghost of Hamlet's father and Fortinbras (mortal enemies) and Hannah is some kind of Barnardo/Francisco/Marcellus/Reynaldo mash-up.

"It's more about the *spirit* of the play," Miss Hammond adds cheerfully. "We want *inspiration* and *creativity*, not a boring traditionalist view."

"Shakespeare will be rolling around in his grave," Mr Bott says, folding his arms laconically. "Screaming in anger and pain."

"Let's try and be positive, shall we?" Miss Hammond snaps at him under her breath. "Why don't we all introduce ourselves briefly and tell everyone why we're so excited to be here?"

There's a long silence.

Then Nat leaps to her feet. "I'm *Natalie*. I'm here because I intend to be famous."

She sits back down again.

"Erm, thank you," Miss Hammond says encouragingly, then switches her gaze to me. "Next?"

"I'm Harriet Manners," I say, standing up and waving awkwardly. "I'm here because..." *of loyalty and an overwhelming sense of guilt.* "I'm a big fan of Shakespeare. Did you know he invented 1,700 words, including *eyeball*, *puking*, *assassination* and *fashionable*?"

Nobody knew that: I can tell from the blank expressions on their faces.

Then it goes round in a circle as the confessions get more and more honest, like some kind of bizarre group-therapy session.

"I'm Mia," Horatio simpers, flushing and standing on one leg. "And…" she glances at Ben and Noah. "I'm here because…"

She starts giggling.

"I don't want to go home," Kira intones, glaring at the clock. "I hate my parents."

"Can my boyfriend come?" Raya asks eagerly, curling her eyelashes round her finger. "He's in Upper Sixth but I'm going to get him a ticket. It's really important he sees me play Ophelia. He likes arty girls."

"I was unaware this was a matchmaking service," Mr Bott says. "How encouraging for England's dramatic future."

"We don't have to do homework, right?" Hannah checks, in a slightly panicked voice. "I mean, that's what I heard."

Nobody has the heart to tell her.

"Does this get us better grades in English?" Laertes asks.

Then there's a shuffly noise as Christopher slinks from his place into the middle of the room with a grumpy expression. He's wearing black from head to toe.

"I'm *Hamlet*," he says gloomily. "And I'm a method actor, so if everyone could refer to me as *Hamlet* from now on, I'd appreciate it. I will also accept *Prince* or *Your Highness of Denmark*."

Mr Bott rolls his eyes. "OK, Christopher."

"Hamlet."

"Christopher."

"Hamlet."

Everyone starts giggling, and then there's a short pause as we all turn to look anxiously at the only remaining person in the room who hasn't confessed yet.

She stares back at us calmly.

"I'm Alexa Roberts, but you all know that. I'm here because I'm really looking forward to helping bring this great play to life from behind the scenes."

Miss Hammond starts clapping delightedly.

"Well, at least *somebody* has the right motives," Mr Bott says drily. "I think that's enough for today. Take the scripts home with you and try to memorise your lines over the rest of the week. We'll see you next Monday. Alexa, you won't need to attend rehearsals until later next week."

"*What*?" Hannah says. "Oh, that is so unfair!"

"And *have fun*!" Miss Hammond chirps, ignoring her. "Remember, this is really a chance to let your stars *twinkle*!"

I put my hand up.

"Stars don't twinkle," I object. "They only *look* like they twinkle because the wavelengths of light are bent by the earth's atmosphere before they reach us."

Every other person in the room except for Nat shoots me a look of disdain.

"I think the scientific term is actually *astronomical scintillation*," I add.

"Well," Miss Hammond says perkily, totally unfazed, "this is a chance to let your dramatic stars astronomically scintillate, then!"

And she claps her hands together and shoos us all out of rehearsal.

18

I spend the rest of the evening learning my lines.

This isn't very hard, because *Hamlet-Mark-Two* is now ten pages long in total. The most famous, critically acclaimed play in the English language is now shorter than an episode of *Hollyoaks*.

My part now consists of the following:

1. "Aye, my lord."
2. "I shall, my lord."
3. "Good, my lord."

Let's just say that Rosencrantz and Guildenstern are very obliging characters and probably don't deserve to get stabbed to death on a boat offstage, which is what ends up happening to them.

Although, on the bright side, at least I don't have to work on my death rattle. I have a feeling I wouldn't be terribly good at it.

I'm just practising walking into a room, bowing and walking out again when my phone starts ringing.

"You know," I say crossly, grabbing it out of my pocket and attempting a small Shakespearean hand flourish in the mirror, "all things considered, you should have let me stay in the cupboard."

"Hello, my little trunkle-monkey," Wilbur laughs.

I blink at the phone. I really have to start looking at the screen before I answer.

"Sorry," I say, flushing slightly. "I thought you were—"

"It's a common mistake, poppet. Nick Hidaka and I are basically twins, separated at birth by thirty years and 100 per cent genetics. I, too, have the cheekbones and jaunty pointed hips of a Renaissance statue."

I smile fondly and sit on the end of the bed. Wilbur really, really doesn't. "Am I in trouble, Wilbur? I'm so sorry. Did *Brink* go mad?"

"*Au contraire*," he giggles. "Do you know how many models stand *Brink* up, poppet-kitten? None. Zilch. Zippo. They think you're playing hard to get. They *love* it."

What? I've never played hard to get in my entire life. "Um… did you tell them where I was?"

"Of course not," Wilbur tinkles. "Can you imagine? 'I'm sorry, but the fresh new face of *Baylee* has got lost at her own modelling agency' isn't the glamorous, sophisticated look Infinity tries to project."

"So what did you tell them instead?"

"I said you had a terribly important and top secret last-minute engagement that may or may not involve Prince Harry."

"Prince *Harry*?"

"You're both ginger. I panicked."

Elizabeth I, Mark Twain, Vincent Van Gogh, Emily Dickinson: all famous redheads. I need to start giving Wilbur little lists or Post-its or something.

Then I abruptly sit up a bit straighter.

"Hang on, Wilbur. What are you saying?"

"I'm saying you got the job, my little phone-charger.

The shoot's next Tuesday: they've arranged it so you can do it after school. It'll be *awesmazing* for your portfolio, chipmunk-cheeks."

A confusing wave washes over me: happiness, pride, anxiety, guilt.

Fear.

The last time I did a fashion shoot, I only managed to survive because Nick was literally holding my hand all the way through.

It's unlikely that this is what *Brink* have in store for me.

"Umm," I say, twisting my duvet cover into nervous little knots. "Do I need to bring anything?"

Wilbur laughs. "Just the usual," he says.

And then he puts the phone down before I can ask exactly what that is.

19

I wait for Nat until Saturday lunchtime.

On Wednesday night, after rehearsals, her mum grounds her for snapping the heel off one of her Jimmy Choos, and Nat's in such a terrible mood I don't have the heart to make it worse.

Or – quite honestly – the courage. My best friend is terrifying when she's angry. And it's quite obvious at school on Thursday and Friday that she hasn't got around to reading the lines.

So instead I tidy my bedroom and get a huge chocolate cake ready so that she can gorge her sorrows in a soothing environment. I've arranged fashion magazines in alphabetical order on my duvet and put all my shoes at right angles to the bed because I know it calms her down.

I've even got a PowerPoint presentation ready, just in case.

It turns out that milking a snake means extracting its venom and is incredibly dangerous, so after a bit more consideration I've taken that off the list.

Then I sit down with a book and wait.

And wait.

Finally, at five minutes to two on Saturday – just as I'm halfway through a cheese sandwich and chapter sixteen of *Great Expectations* – Annabel shouts up the stairs:

"Harriet? Sweetheart, Nat's here to see y—"

And my bedroom door smashes open and Nat bursts in, hair and arms and coat and bag everywhere, like a hand-grenade made out of girl.

"What. The. Hell," she yells loudly, throwing the bits of pink paper on the bed in front of me.

I stop chewing.

"I'm a *skull*? My acting career is going to start by replacing a prop they could have got out of the physics cupboard?"

"I think they keep the plastic skeleton in the biology cupboard, actually," I say, putting my sandwich down. "Nat, I didn't know how to tell you."

"*Ugh*," she says, flopping on the bed next to me. I silently cut a slice of cake and hand it to her. "I've been through the whole script three times, Harriet. Apparently Chris just has to hold my face and talk nonsense at me. That's not a *role*. That's a really bad date."

She rams a slice of chocolate cake into her mouth and starts chewing frantically. I rub her arm and gently nudge *Grazia* forward with one of my toes.

"You know," she says with her mouth full, "this is why the British acting industry is in meltdown. No wonder Emma Watson has to play everything. They just don't give anyone else a chance."

"They're fools," I say fiercely, shaking my head. "Silly, silly fools."

"What am I going to do?"

"*Well*," I say, jumping up and pressing a button on my laptop. "I'm glad you asked, because I think there are some options that might be—"

"Maybe I could be Raya's understudy. Maybe if she

75

accidentally gets sick, I can be Ophelia and..."

Oh dear. Nat has been known to make people sick with prawns when she wants them out of the way.

"I'm not sure Raya's allergic to shellfish, Nat."

"She has to be allergic to *something*." I lift an eyebrow at her. "Don't look at me like that, Harriet. I don't mean *deathly* allergic. Just a bit sweaty and shaky for a few hours. I'm not going to *kill* anyone."

"I'm not sure you can monitor that scientifically enough for it to be morally acceptable."

Nat sighs.

"*So*," I continue, pressing another button so that a colourful image of a water slide appears on the white wall opposite, "I was thinking that..."

Nat's chewing more carefully.

"No," she says slowly. "Actually, it's OK. I'm going to be a *skull*. I'm going to be the best skull that has ever existed. I'm going to be so great that somebody writes a spin-off all about Yorick and they ask me to play her."

"Him."

"Whatever." Nat puts the chocolate cake down. "I'm going to make this play *my own*."

I beam at her. "That's the spirit," I say, clicking another button. A huge photo of a teddy bear shines on the wall. "And if you need a Plan B, there's always—"

"There is no Plan B," Nat says darkly, staring at the wall. "There is only Plan A."

I look at her in consternation. She's starting to sound like the baddie in a Batman trailer.

"Well..."

Nat shakes her head. "I just have to throw myself into

it, that's all. We've got a rehearsal on Monday night and I'm grounded for the rest of the weekend, but on Tuesday can we do some research on famous skulls? It might help me get in the *zone*."

"*Oooh*," I say happily, shutting my laptop. *This* is more like it. "Definitely. There's Geronimo's skull: that got stolen from his grave in 1918. And Damien Hirst's skull, covered in diamonds, and then the crystal skulls from the ancient Mesoamerican civilisation, thought to have had supernatural powers and…"

I stop. *Sugar cookies*.

"I can't," I say after a small pause. "I have, an… erm… photo shoot with *Brink* magazine."

"*Brink*?" Nat says, picking up one of the magazines on my bed and holding it up. "As in Brink *Brink*?"

I nod guiltily. "I think you just say it once, Nat."

There's the tiniest of pauses while Nat goes white, then pink, then a faint purple, then a strange kind of green.

I watch my best friend change colour like Violet Beauregard from *Charlie and the Chocolate Factory* with a sinking, guilty stomach. Ten years. Ten years of pulling on her hands and feet to make her taller, and with one stumble into a table full of hats I fall straight into her dream and leave her standing behind.

"I'm so sorry," I say in a tiny voice. "It's really bad timing."

Nat shakes herself. "Don't be ridiculous, Harriet," she says, putting her arm around me and slowly returning to normal colour. "That's *amazing*. I'm so proud of you."

It's suddenly difficult to swallow. This is what it's all about. Not a play. Not a photo shoot. Not a boy or a girl or a skull or a cupboard.

A friend.

The kind that will happily hurt for you, and you'll hurt for in return.

"But you could come with me?" I offer tentatively. "I mean, if you want to?"

I'm not sure if that's a good idea or like eating steak in front of a starving lion.

Nat's eyes widen. "Could I? Really? Are you kidding? You don't mind?"

I beam at her.

"Of course I don't, Nat. It'll be great to have you with me."

Because it will be.

Maybe somebody will be there to hold my hand after all.

20

Now, I know quite a lot about Shakespeare.

I know that:

- He used 31,534 different words to write 37 plays and 154 sonnets.
- 1,700 of those words were made up.
- He invented the expressions 'wild goose chase', 'in a pickle', 'one fell swoop' and 'all of a sudden'.
- The only remaining example of Shakespeare's actual writing is his own name…
- Which was never once spelled *William Shakespeare*.

None of this is of any help during our first rehearsal.

In fact, it almost definitely makes things worse.

"Now," Miss Hammond says as we stand in an awkward, shuffling circle. "The key thing to remember about any play is that it's not about the *words*."

"Uh-huh," Mr Bott says from where he's reading a book in the corner. "Shame nobody told William Shakespeare."

Miss Hammond gives him a brief look.

"A *play*," she says, turning back to us and swooshing her hands together, bracelets a-jangling, "is first and foremost about *expression*. About *emotion*. About *feeling* the story, in your heart, in your bones, in your very *soul*."

"And then conveying that story with words."

"Thank you, Mr Bott," Miss Hammond says, turning her back on him. "So let's put those silly words aside for today, shall we? It's time to let ourselves be. To loosen up and let those beautiful emotions just pour out of us like sunshine."

I glance briefly at Mr Bott.

I'm with him on this one. The sun's power is about 386 billion billion megawatts. If it was coming out of us, we'd definitely know about it.

"I'm confused," Mia whispers. "Does this mean we're doing mime?"

"Everybody crouch on the floor!" Miss Hammond cries, spreading her recently henna-tattooed hands out. "Quickly!"

"You've got to be kidding me," Nat snaps in a low voice. "These are brand-new trousers."

"Hamlet doesn't *crouch*," Christopher complains, folding his arms. He's still wearing a black jumper with a turtleneck. "Hamlet is *royalty*."

"She said *everybody*," Mr Bott snaps loudly. "Get on the floor immediately, Christopher, and stop referring to yourself in the third person."

Christopher grumbles his way into a small huddled position. "No wonder I end up killing everyone," he mutters under his breath.

Miss Hammond smiles enthusiastically at us.

"*Now*," she says. "Curl up *tightly*. You are a bud from which a delicate flower is going to grow. Tap deep, deep into the soil and find the emotion of your character. Draw it into you like water."

I glance across at Nat from where I'm tucked up with

my chin on my knees. She mimes sucking from a straw like a little pet gerbil, and we both start sniggering quietly into our trousers.

"Now uncurl your leaves, slowly, and reach up to the light of emotional truth."

Everybody starts awkwardly sticking their hands out and waving them around like fish fins.

"Miss," Raya complains, "Noah's leaves keep touching my leaves."

"Keep your leaves to yourself, Noah," Mr Bott says sharply.

"That's it," Miss Hammond smiles, wiggling her fingers as she wanders between us with her necklaces jingling. "Now stretch *up, up, up* and *grow* into the characters you are meant to be. Really *feel* it."

I *can* really feel it. My thigh muscles are nowhere near strong enough to be in this kind of squatting position for as long as they have been.

I collapse back on the floor.

Nat starts giggling again from where she's waving her arms around like somebody playing the tambourine in the sixties.

"*Grow*," she whispers at me, giggling. "*Grow*, little bud."

"I think I'm more of a sprout," I whisper back, snorting slightly.

"Now *stand*," Miss Hammond says, twirling in a circle. "And reach your full potential. You are a tree. You are *strength* and *courage*. You are *amazing*."

"I thought we were flowers?" I say, clambering to my feet. "How can we be trees too? We don't have the necessary fibrous tissue."

"You're a flower that turned into a tree," Mr Bott says drily. "Don't question the process, Harriet. Just accept that biologically it makes no sense and do it."

I nod sheepishly. "Sorry, sir."

We all stand and wave our branches around awkwardly for a few minutes as we 'access the honesty of our spiritual fictional selves'.

"OK," Miss Hammond says brightly as Kira starts moaning that her trunk is hurting and Noah's leaves are getting too enthusiastic again. "That's it! Now shake it out! Doesn't that feel great?"

Four people lie straight down on the floor again. "I've got a headache, Miss," Ben complains. "I think I didn't drink enough imaginary water."

"Would you like to do a straight read-through now, Miss Hammond?" Mr Bott says calmly. "Or will the silly words just ruin everything?"

Miss Hammond looks around the room with happy pink cheeks. "I think we've done enough hard work for today, don't you? It's clear that everyone has really *connected emotionally* with who they are, and that's what's important."

Mr Bott stands up and puts his book down.

"Oh, absolutely. When the headmaster asks why *Hamlet* has turned into a silent botanical garden, that's what I'll tell him."

And he puts his coat on and walks out of the room, slamming the door behind him.

"Can we go now, Miss?" Kira says in a bored voice.

"Absolutely," Miss Hammond says brightly. "Go

home and enjoy this lovely spring evening! Excellent job, everyone! The Bard would be so incredibly proud of you all!"

And I have to be honest.

Of all the things I know about Shakespeare, that fact is *definitely* not one of them.

21

Honestly, the next day at school is a bit of a struggle.

This is partly because my leg muscles hurt, partly because I'm now carrying my pencil case and books round in Annabel's old leather briefcase, and partly because Nat is so excited about the *Brink* shoot she can't stop asking questions.

"Where's it going to be?" she asks during registration. "Who's the photographer? Who's the stylist? What's the *theme*?"

"When's it published?" she asks at morning break.

"How much are you being paid?" she asks at lunch.

Afternoon break: "Can I take photos of the photos?"

Before physics: "Do you think my blue dress and gold heels will be OK?"

After physics: "What about my hair? Do you think it should be down or in a topknot or…? Where are you going?"

"Away," I say tiredly. "You're my best friend in the world and I love you, Nat, but you're kind of doing my head in."

Seriously: after today I think I finally understand how irritating I am when I don't stop demanding answers from everybody all the time.

Especially when they don't actually know any of them.

"Sorry," Nat says, racing after me. "Sorry, sorry. It's

just… This is my *first fashion shoot,* Harriet. It's like… being Buzz Aldrin on the moon or something."

"Neil Armstrong was the first man on the moon, Nat."

"Exactly. I'm the second one. I'm all like, 'Hey, Neil, what's it like out there?' and Neil's all like, 'Come out and see for yourself, wuss!'"

I laugh. "I'm not Armstrong, Nat. I don't know any more than you do."

"Sure you do. Have they given you a call sheet? I wonder if they've issued a pull letter, or if the shoot will be tethered, or if they've got an LOR. Either way, you'll end up with an *amazing* tear sheet."

I look at Nat blankly for a few seconds.

Njerep is a language found in Nigeria, and there are only four people left in the world who speak it. She'd have had more luck being understood if she'd just opted for that instead.

"Correction, I know a *lot less* than you. Like, significantly."

Nat laughs. "Want to meet at the train station? I've got to get my stuff together. I'm taking a notepad and a pencil and a camera and a spare needle and thread, just in case, and—"

This is possibly the first time in our entire lives that Nat has ever sounded like a geek.

I *knew* there was a point where we'd eventually cross over. Like some kind of Venn diagram between cool and nerd: there's always a point of intersection somewhere.

"I'll meet you at five," I say, cramming a bit of doughnut I just found in my satchel into my mouth.

My best friend stares at my doughnut, and then at the

jam dripping on to my school jumper.

"I can't believe I spent ten years eating celery," she says sadly, holding her hand out. "Such a waste."

I give her the rest of it and grimace in agreement.

I don't believe in a cosmic plan, but if I did, it definitely has quite a cruel sense of humour.

22

The *Brink* photo shoot is being held in an abandoned building.

And when I say *abandoned*, I mean this very literally.

There are no windows. Some of the walls have fallen down and a couple of the doors are missing chunks. There's rubble on the floor, bits of plasterboard strewn haphazardly around and to get to the second floor we have to tentatively clamber up a rickety iron spiral staircase that seems to be hanging on by its fingertips.

"It's so *cool*," Nat says with a happy sigh. "So *edgy*."

I look around sceptically.

It's edgy, all right. There's definitely some kind of health and safety legislation being broken here. The only reason I'm allowed to do this shoot without my parents is that I promised them Wilbur would be here as well as Nat and I'd be back by 8pm.

If one of these *edges* results in me getting tetanus, Annabel is going to sue everyone.

"I'm not entirely sure we got the right addres—"

"Pumpkin-koala and her biff!" a voice cries from behind a wall. "You made it! I was starting to think you might have vanished into the ether like my Uncle Bert in the sixties."

Nat quickly straightens her dress out. "How do I look?" she whispers urgently as Wilbur emerges from

behind a disintegrating pile of bricks in a yellow jumpsuit, like some kind of neon urban butterfly.

"Perfect," I whisper back.

"My little dolly-mixture," Wilbur says, grabbing Nat's hand and bending into a deep bow. "How cute are you? It's a rhetorical question. You're as cute as the tiniest button in the entire world."

Nat beams so hard her entire face looks like it's about to crack and fall off.

"Thanks very much."

"As for you..." My agent turns to me and looks me up and down. "Is that jam, darling-frog, or have you been a little bit murdered on the journey?"

In hindsight, I should probably have changed out of my doughnut-encrusted school uniform. "I had some pretty important homework to do," I explain.

"I *love* it!" Wilbur giggles. "So expressive! Strawberry or raspberry?"

"Raspberry."

"Absolute classic! And the sugar looks like tiny edible sparkles! Genius!"

He claps his hands and then grabs us both by the shoulders and drags us around the partition.

And everything abruptly changes.

Gone is the mess and broken up bricks; the faint veil of dust and pieces of randomly placed cement have totally disappeared. In their place is a haven of calm and cleanliness.

Everything is bright white.

The floors are white, the ceilings are white, the walls are white. In the middle is an enormous white piece of paper strung from the ceiling and draped halfway across the room – so unmarked it looks like fresh snow first thing in the morning.

And in the middle of the whiteness are enormous shiny silver lights and black boxes and shiny gold and silver circles and little black umbrellas.

"Oh my God," Nat sighs under her breath. "This is *exactly* what heaven looks like."

She has a point. If you listen hard enough, I'm pretty sure you can hear fashion-y harp music.

"Come!" Wilbur says, dragging us both into a small separate room with an enormous mirror surrounded by tiny white lights. There are clothes everywhere: on racks, on tables, on chairs. Shoes are lined up like a strategic army on the floor, handbags are dangling delicately from coat hangers like little monkeys and there's a tiered trolley exploding with cosmetics.

I swallow hard.

Apparently rats lack the brain circuits required for throwing up: the nerves in their mouths, throats and shoulders aren't developed enough for them to be sick.

This may be the first time in my life I've ever wished I was a rat.

Nat makes a small whimpering sound.

"*Gucci,*" she whispers reverently, running into the room and holding her hand out as if she's trying to levitate things with her mind. "Prada. Mulberry. Armani. Ralph Lauren." She's starting to hyperventilate. "*Wow-wow-wow-wow – is that an actual Chloé handbag?*"

Wilbur smiles at Nat, gently leads her to a chair and hands her a glass of water.

Then he turns back to me. "So we've got a *real* treat in store for you today, my little cashew-nut cake."

I nod nervously. "Mmm."

"This is going to be so fresh it's still going to be flopping around on the floor, gasping for air. *Comprende*?"

"Not really," I admit.

A woman in a white vest top and black skinny jeans charges into the room. "Carrots!" she shouts in a raspy voice.

Then, without another word, she charges back out again.

I look around the room in confusion – there doesn't appear to be a lot of vegetation in here – and then flush. Is she talking to *me*?

Carrots?

That's not a very polite way to greet somebody you've never met before.

"*Was that*…?" Every feature on Nat's face is now an O. "Was that *Adrianna Bell*?"

"It certainly was," Wilbur says, beaming. "The one and only. Now can you see what I'm talking about?"

"*Oh, wow*," Nat says fervently, clasping her hands together and looking at the ceiling. "Harriet, you are so *lucky*."

I smile tentatively.

I know a lot of things. I know that emus lay emerald-coloured eggs. I know that the ingredient that makes Brussels sprouts bitter is cyanide and that a raindrop that falls into the Thames will pass through the bodies of eight people before it reaches the sea.

But I have zero idea who Adrianna Bell is.

And I can't help thinking that right now I'd trade in every single one of those facts for just some vague idea of what she's going to expect me to do next.

23

Here are some interesting facts about orange:

1. The fruit came before the colour.
2. It derives from the Arabic word *naranji*, which became *narange* when the fruit arrived in England in the fourteenth century, eventually dropped the *n* before changing the *a* to an *o*.
3. It takes fifty glasses of water to grow enough oranges to make one glass of orange juice.
4. Orange was first used as the name for a colour in 1542.

These are all things I tell the make-up artist, because I am being *covered* in it.

Over the following hour, my eyes are painted bright orange. My lips are rendered bright orange. My nails are orange, and my cheeks are powdered with a faint orange blush. My enormous fake eyelashes are orange feathers with tiny bits of orange sequin stuck to the edges, and a line of orange diamante has been glued in a long, smooth curve down my back and neck.

My hair's a shade of orange too, but that's nothing to do with the stylist. That's down to the lottery my parents played with their recessive MC1R genes.

Finally, I'm put in a teeny tiny orange shift dress that

hangs straight down in a soft, floaty sack shape.

"You look *amazing*," Nat sighs, clapping her hands. She's spent the last hour hovering around the stylist like a moth around a lightbulb, asking questions like, "So a *brush* is the best way to apply foundation?" and, "Is primer *really* worth the investment?"

"In the Chinese art of *feng shui*, orange is the colour of purpose and organisation," I say, leaning curiously towards my reflection in the mirror. "I definitely feel very regulated."

Then I lean a little bit closer.

The clumsy schoolgirl has gone; the lashless eyes have gone; the freckles have gone. The only thing I really recognise is my pointy nose, and even that appears to have been reshaped slightly with clever application of dark smudges.

"Carrots!" Adrianna belts through the wall. "We're ready for you, Carrots!"

Seriously.

Adrianna might apparently be an award-winning, celebrity-beloved photographer, but she may need to work on her people skills.

That is not the best way to win a teenager over.

"Coming!" I call nervously as Nat high-fives me and I make my way cautiously in bare feet back into the white room.

And then I stop.

The white sheet hanging from the ceiling has disappeared, and in its place is a pale orange background with large paintings of bright orange carrots all over it.

Root vegetable carrots.

The kind my dad keeps putting in casseroles even though they go all soggy and every single bit of vitamin C is totally heat-destroyed in the process, rendering them completely pointless.

"There she is," Adrianna fixes her gaze on me. "My carrot." She grabs my face between her hands so hard it's squidged into a potato shape. "I knew you were a carrot the minute I saw you, Harriet. You're so carrot it's crazy."

I open and shut my mouth a few times.

"Excuse me?"

"There was no other choice," she says happily. "I saw your photo and I was like, *wham*. There's Carrot! Call off the hunt! Nobody else will do!"

I frown at the set, and then look down at my outfit. Things are starting to fall into place.

Not quickly, or with any real sense, but logically nonetheless.

"Have a look," she says, dragging me over to the laptop. "We've already done Raspberry and Banana. Pear was a total nightmare – such a diva – and Broccoli was a bit rigid, but overall it's gone really well. *Brink* are going to love it."

She clicks a few buttons, and bright images start flicking on the screen.

A beautiful girl with pale yellow hair and bright yellow make-up, standing against a backdrop of shiny bananas. The profile of a boy with pale skin and a green mohawk, against a backdrop of green florets. Bright pink lips and a pink afro, and another girl with heavy black eyeliner and a sharp green bob.

Who knew high fashion could be so literal?

94

Not to mention nutritious. We look like some kind of NHS poster campaign.

Still totally silent, I'm walked gently over to the middle of the backdrop and left to shift awkwardly from side to side while Adrianna fiddles with a few buttons and moves some lights around.

"Doesn't she have shoes?" she says, looking up and frowning.

"I wasn't sure which ones you wanted," the stylist calls from the back room. "We've got the orange Miu Mius or the orange McQueens."

Two hands hold them up through the door. They both look insanely high. Unless they want to shoot me lying on the floor, I'm not entirely sure either is a good option.

"Umm," I start, swallowing hard, and then Nat appears with flushed cheeks.

"Or *green* ones?" she suggests, holding out a pair of neon kitten heels. "These Blahniks would work, wouldn't they? I mean, carrots have green leaves, don't they?"

There's a silence.

"Who's this?" Adrianna asks nobody in particular, turning around slowly.

Nat straightens and I see her go into war mode: chin up, eyes narrowed. "I'm Natalie Grey," she says defiantly.

"Well, give the model those heels."

Nat's cheeks go bright pink with happiness, and she hesitates for a few seconds before running towards me.

I could kiss her. They're only about two inches high.

"Thought you might find these a bit easier," she whispers under her breath as I take the shoes from her and slip them on my feet.

"I love you," I whisper back.

"Ditto," she winks at me.

"Right," Adrianna says as Wilbur starts doing some kind of celebratory t'ai chi in the background. "Let's get on with it, shall we?"

And we do.

24

Amazingly, the shoot is a success.

Apparently all I have to do is *harness my inner carrot*, and I don't want to be vain, but it's easier than I thought.

I swing my handbag around and shift from side to side. I stare blankly into space as if I've forgotten what it is I'm about to say. I hop into the air with my leg out.

I turn around and peer over my shoulder so that the diamante on my back is twisted into a zig zag.

And, as I crumple and stretch, pivot and expand (only falling over twice), I can't help wondering if Adrianna has been in cahoots with Miss Hammond this whole time. I'm basically now a trained vegetation impressionist.

Finally, Adrianna gives a whoop, tells me we're all finished, and I'm wiped clean and de-orangified.

Then Nat and I make our journey home.

"You know," she says thoughtfully as we finally reach the bench on the corner at the end of my road, "that wasn't what I thought it would be like at *all*."

She's been quiet the whole way: undoing and redoing the laces on her boots for no apparent reason.

"Me neither," I say with feeling.

I'm not sure what I expected from the glamorous world of modelling this time, but it definitely wasn't to be the most colourful portion of Five A Day.

"I mean," Nat says, frowning, "I've wanted to model forever, Harriet. Like… *always*. But, actually *being* there… I'm not sure I could do it."

"Oh, you could," I say vehemently. "It's not exactly rocket science. Apparently a human can only express four basic emotions, and modelling doesn't involve *any* of them."

She uses one of them up to smile at me.

"OK, I'm not sure I'd *want* to do it. This sounds weird, but it feels like something's kind of… gone. Evaporated. Or died, somehow. I feel lighter than I have in ages. Months. *Years*."

I assess her for a few seconds.

"I think you're the same weight, Nat. Possibly heavier: I'm afraid that doughnut will have digested by now and gone straight to your hips."

Then I stick my tongue out.

"Whatever. Yours has gone straight to your stomach." Nat points at the jam smear still on my jumper and laughs. Then she grabs my arm and leans into my shoulder. "Thank you. I mean it."

"What for?"

"Showing me what I couldn't see before."

And with a little kiss on my cheek, Nat smiles a little bit harder and bounces back to her house with her shiny dark hair bobbing behind her.

25

Rehearsals start in earnest the next day.

Let's just say that Mr Bott and Miss Hammond obviously had an altercation in the staff room, because, when we meet the next afternoon, our drama teacher is very quiet and our English teacher is sitting on a chair in the centre of the room with his arms crossed.

Traditionally, tribes all over the world have used ornamentation to publicly declare their social standing. From the drastically reduced quantity of necklaces Miss Hammond has on, it looks like she's decided to do that too.

"Now," Mr Bott says sharply, "would I be right in assuming that you've *loosened up* enough to start actually practising *Hamlet*?"

A groan goes round the room.

"Remember," Miss Hammond says, flapping her arms, "it's been edited down *significantly*."

"Yes," Mr Bott says. "And I'm sure if Shakespeare had seen your auditions, he would have done that too." He sighs. "Why don't we start with 'Long live the King' and go from there?"

We proceed to limp, jerk and stagger our way through *Hamlet* with such wooden rigidity, I think we may have harnessed our inner trees a little bit too enthusiastically.

In the meantime, I get on with some physics revision.

There's only so much focus you need to say, "Yes, your Majesty" every few pages, and I use the rest of my time to learn about the varying lengths of electromagnetic waves.

Mr Bott doesn't like it, but he can't really say anything: Yorick is reading *Vogue* and Ophelia keeps looking in her mirror "to see what shape my lips make when I talk".

Finally, it's Nat's turn.

I put my book down and look up curiously.

Christopher stands up and walks in circles a few times, with his white school shirt sticking out from under his black jumper like an untidy penguin. Then he kneels down on the floor where Nat is patiently lying, perfectly still.

"Alas, poor Yorick," he says in a pained voice to Mia, holding Nat's face gently in his hands. "I knew him, Horatio. A fellow of infinite jest, of most excellent fancy. Here hung those lips that I have kissed I know not how oft."

And then he bends down and kisses Nat on the lips.

I've never seen anyone move so fast. Especially not somebody pretending to be dead.

"What the…!" she shouts, jumping up and vigorously rubbing her mouth on her jumper sleeve. "That is *not* in the script!"

"I was *improvising*," Christopher shrugs. "I was feeling the moment."

"I'll *improvise your face*," Nat yells, physically launching herself at him. "I'll improvise it into next week!"

Miss Hammond quickly steps between them.

"OK. Christopher, I don't think that Hamlet would go around kissing skulls just dug out of the ground, do you?"

"He might," Christopher says obstinately. "We don't

100

know what people from Denmark did four hundred years ago."

"I will *bite* you," Nat shouts, straining forwards. "Touch me with your lips again and you will *lose* them."

"Fine, fine," he says, holding up his hands. "A pity though. You're clearly not a committed artist like me."

Nat glares at him. "Oh, you need *committing* all right, buddy," she growls, and then slowly lies back down on the floor once more.

Christopher clears his throat and continues with his monologue.

Then Raya is carried clumsily in by me, Hannah, Noah and Rob, each clutching a shin or a wrist or a bit of shoulder. It doesn't seem to bother anyone that – thanks to character blending – the pallbearers at Ophelia's funeral are three dead people and a priest.

We plonk her awkwardly on the ground to an unmistakable "Owww!" from Hamlet's dead girlfriend.

"Lay her i'th'earth," Max says stiffly. "And from her fair and unpolluted flesh may violets spring."

"Sweets to the sweet," Kira agrees in a bored voice, throwing bits of tissue at Ophelia in lieu of flowers. "Farewell."

Then it all kicks off: Hamlet and Laertes have a bit of a scuffle in the grave, which results in Ophelia getting her finger trod on and we drag her off to a corner while she's still complaining, so that the final showdown can commence.

Ten minutes later, there's a pile of dead students lying on the floor with varying levels of commitment to no longer existing.

Ophelia's filing a nail, Laertes and King Claudius are whispering to each other, Gertrude's foot keeps twitching and Hamlet's clutching his own throat, which I'm pretty sure wouldn't be possible in the last throes of rigor mortis.

I've been forced to lie down too, even though I point out quite crossly that I'm supposed to be on my way to France right now, and it seems unlikely they would bother to drag my body all the way back to Denmark just for this scene. I'd definitely have been thrown overboard.

"It adds *impact*," Miss Hammond whispers. "The more bodies at the end, the sadder it will be. Actually," and she waves in Rob, Hannah, Noah and Nat, "you might as well come and lie down too."

"I'm not even *dead*, Miss," Hannah complains. "I'm, like, one of the only survivors."

"Nobody will remember that," Miss Hammond assures her.

Hannah sighs and lies down with the rest of us.

"Oh, I DIE," Christopher shouts, choking on his own hands. "The potent poison quite o'ercrows my spirit. The rest is *silence!!!*"

And he rattles, flops around a few times like a fish dragged out of the sea, and then lies down with his hand over his face.

"Yes," Mr Bott says flatly, standing up. "The rest is silence, indeed. We can only hope. Thank you, everyone."

There's a slow clapping from the other side of the room and I sit up just in time to see Alexa, sitting in a darkened corner, like some kind of enormous, too-intelligent spider.

And not in a cute, *Charlotte's Web* kind of way.

I can imagine her spelling out words in her web, but

they definitely wouldn't be encouraging ones.

"That was *terrific*," she smiles as most of us slowly sit up and rub our eyes. I think Noah's actually fallen asleep. "I've got so many great ideas already for how to *enhance* this production."

Honestly, I'm not entirely sure how she could possibly make it worse. But I have a feeling that she's going to give it a good shot regardless.

She's reliable like that.

"See you there," Alexa says, bowing low. "*Especially* you, Harriet Manners."

And as she backs out of the room, still making fixed eye contact, I can't help thinking I should probably be on a boat to France in real life too.

When Nick rings me half an hour later, the conversation doesn't go quite as he expects it to.

"I'm sorry, Harriet," he says in a low voice. "I've been called to Milan for a shoot on Monday, which means I'm not going to make it back in time for your play. I'm totally gutted."

There's a long silence.

"I've tried really hard to get out of it," he continues, "but I'm on contract and there's nothing I can do and…"

He stops.

"Are you OK?" he checks. "You haven't smashed your phone really quietly, have you? Or eaten it?"

I laugh.

I've been quickly weighing up the pros and cons of not having Nick there to support me versus not having Nick there to see me humiliated.

Especially you, Harriet Manners.

Yup: that does it.

"Nope," I decide happily. "In fact, I'm elated. Ecstatic. Overjoyed and tickled pink. Like a dog with two tails. As pleased as punch." I pause. "Or something a bit less rude," I amend quickly. "Should I start that again?"

"Yes please," Nick laughs. "I'm assuming your dad will make a video?"

Yes: it's safe to say my dad will be making a video. He made a video of the dog getting a haircut last week. There doesn't seem to be much quality control going on at the moment. Thus the joys of unemployment.

"I'm afraid so."

"Then I'll look forward to watching that when I'm back. We can make an evening of it."

I think about it briefly.

"Sure," I lie.

The National Security Agency managed to destroy years' worth of telephone and internet records. I can definitely destroy an incriminating video in the time it takes Nick to fly home from Italy.

26

The Hamletians — as Miss Hammond has started calling us — practise for the rest of the week.

We practise at lunch, at break-times, after school and before registration. I hear Noah and Mia running through their lines in the corridors outside biology, and Raya muttering in a decidedly heartsick manner in the school canteen.

With some prodding, we even come in, reluctantly, on Saturday afternoon for a quick dress rehearsal as well.

And — to my total surprise — we slowly get better.

I mean, none of us is going to get a call from the Royal Shakespeare Company at any stage in the near future, but we're not *that* bad any more.

A slug has its bottom in its head. Let's just say you make the best of what you've got.

By the time the open evening itself arrives, the level of general excitement is dangerously high. Ben and Noah keep fist-bumping each other outside the hall, Christopher is skulking around, darkly muttering, "Frailty, thy name is woman!" at every girl who walks past, and Max keeps lobbing a little balloon of red food dye into the air.

"You know," he says chirpily, catching it again, "I'm actually quite looking forward to getting stabbed to death now."

Even Nat's spirits have lifted enormously.

She turned up on Saturday with a big bundle of clothes: a beautiful white, floaty dress for Raya, a full length blue dress for Kira, a range of soldier's jackets and waistcoats for the boys and a velvet coat for me.

"Where did you get these?!" Miss Hammond asked incredulously as Nat held up her own black, shiny catsuit.

Nat shrugged. "Charity shops, sewing machine, Mum's attic."

I looked again at the dress Raya was spinning around in, which was almost definitely Nat's mum's wedding dress. It was probably a good thing my best friend was dead throughout the play, because she wouldn't be alive for long after it either.

While we get ready in an empty girls' changing room, I take a moment to glance sideways at my best friend.

Nat's cheeks are getting pinker by the second, her eyes are getting brighter, and her lips are getting more and more rigid.

She managed to convince Miss Hammond that a "subtle skull look" was "the best way to approach this, stylistically," and now has slightly pale foundation and dark, smoky eye make-up. With her catsuit, she looks less like the cranial bone of somebody's head and more like Sandy from the final scene in *Grease*.

Which I'm guessing is kind of the point.

I study her face suspiciously. The last time Nat had an expression like this, we were seven and she had just let the class hamster out of the cage because our teacher wouldn't let her take it home for the weekend.

"What are you up to, Natalie?"

Nat tosses her head. "Huh?" she says, looking at a

space somewhere behind my head. "Hmm? What? What on earth do you mean?"

Then she opens her eyes unnaturally wide.

Yup: she's up to something. That's just what she looked like ten minutes after Bobby was found in the car park outside, hiding under a car tyre, nibbling his paws anxiously.

"You're not planning on... *doing* anything, are you?"

"I don't know what you're talking about," Nat says indignantly, and stalks back over to the mirror to fluff up her hair. "Really, Harriet. What kind of girl do you think I am?"

I'm just trying to find a way to politely answer that question when there's a loud scream from the corridor.

"No no no no no no *no*," somebody starts shouting. "No no no nononono. This *can't be happening*."

Nat and I glance at each other and then run quickly into the hallway. Within seconds, every member of the cast is standing in a horrified, silent circle.

"Oh, good gracious!" Mr Bott says, putting his hand across his mouth.

Raya is sitting in a crumpled heap on the floor: white dress rumpled around her, phone clutched tightly in her hand. Her hair is everywhere, her eyes are pink and swollen and her cheeks are wet and shiny.

"No," she keeps murmuring at her lap. "*No. No. No.*"

Miss Hammond appears in a flurry of lace and beads and quickly bends down. "Raya," she says. "Sweetheart, what's happened?"

Raya looks up: enormous deer eyelashes soggy and sparkling. "H-h-h," she starts. "H-h-h."

"Take a deep breath," Miss Hammond reminds her, patting a jangling hand on her shoulder (the bracelets have reappeared in force for tonight). "Let those emotions wash over you like a cleansing tide."

Raya nods and closes her eyes. "H-h-h-he *dumped* me."

Then she throws her head back and starts howling at the ceiling.

"Oh, thank goodness," Mr Bott says in genuine relief. "I thought it was something important."

Miss Hammond scowls at him, but not before Raya has jumped off the floor. Her eyes are wild, and there appears to be a bit of face paint stuck in her eyebrow. "You *don't understand because you're a man*," she screams at him. "My heart is *broken*! I will never recover! *Never!*"

The circle of concerned onlookers is slowly starting to move away, the way you'd inch backwards if you discovered a velociraptor in your bathroom.

One of the boys appears to be whistling quietly.

"Well…" Mr Bott says, clearing his throat. I've never seen anyone look more uncomfortable. "That's not actually true, Raya. You're fifteen…"

"*Sixteen.*"

"Exactly. And you'll… erm… love again." He clears his throat. "Probably. I mean, that's not guaranteed, but probably."

Raya's head drops and she starts wailing into her lap again.

"Now," Miss Hammond says, bending down next to her and giving Mr Bott the look of death. "Come on, Raya. You know what *really* makes a man regret dumping someone? *Seeing them on stage looking beautiful and word-perfect.*"

There's a little sniffle while Raya considers this. "I do look quite pretty, don't I?"

"Absolutely," Miss Hammond says a little too fiercely. Humans shed on average 121 pints of tears in a lifetime and Raya's face looks like it's tried to get them all out of the way at once. "Be strong, and go show him what he's missing. *Do the play.*"

Raya tips her head to the side and then wipes her nose on the sleeve of Nat's mum's wedding dress.

"OK," she says quietly, standing up on wobbly legs like a toddler. "Do you think it'll make him want me back?"

"Of course," Miss Hammond says after a few seconds of hesitation. In fairness, Ophelia's not exactly the most attractive Shakespearean heroine: insane girls who drown themselves while singing about flowers never tend to be.

"Then that's what I'll do," Raya says, lifting her chin slightly.

Everyone takes one cautious step closer.

"Right," Mr Bott says, abruptly. "Disaster has been averted. We've got twenty minutes before everyone starts turning up, so let's make the most of them, shall we?"

And the countdown begins.

27

Last time I was on a stage was in Moscow.

It was an old, expensive gilt theatre, with a plush red carpet, velvet seats with gold carvings and an enormous crystal chandelier hanging from an ornate ceiling. There was a catwalk running down the middle of a circular room, a plethora of thin, beautiful, semi-naked Russian models running around backstage, and my father, embarrassing me from a seat at the back.

At least some things never change.

As I stick my head out from behind the dusty green curtains on the wooden, scratched school stage and stare at the growing crowd accumulating on little plastic chairs, I can see my dad: visible like a flame in the night.

Less than two per cent of the world have red hair and in situations like this it can be quite handy.

"Hey, Harriet!" he shouts, standing up and prodding Annabel. My stepmother is wearing her navy blue suit, and there appears to be some kind of pizza balanced on top of her bump. "She's there, Annabel!" he shouts, waving energetically. "Can you see her? Sticking out from behind that curtain!"

Sugar cookies.

I sometimes forget that I have glow-in-the-dark red hair too.

I duck and watch Annabel roll her eyes, drag Dad back

into a seated position and tell him to behave himself. Then they lean over and start chatting animatedly to a very pretty woman with dark hair and a face exactly like Nat's, except modified slightly by twenty years and plastic surgery.

"Oooh, your mum's here too," I whisper to Nat in excitement.

Then I stop.

Nat's breathing in and out of a paper bag, and her face is now totally bone white. I don't think she needed make-up after all. She's looking remarkably skull-like.

"*Don't*," she whispers, breathing faster. "Harriet, I can't… I don't… I need to *focus*."

I nod in an understanding kind of way. If I wasn't essentially playing a glorified extra, I probably would as well.

Instead, I put my arm around her.

"You're going to be great," I say as Raya wanders past, weeping quietly into the crook of her arm.

"Maybe," Nat says, swallowing. "Whatever happens, you'll be there, right?"

What does she mean, *whatever happens*?

I *knew* it. If there's a hamster anywhere in the vicinity, he's definitely in trouble. "Of course. I'm behind you a hundred per cent."

"And I'm behind *you*, Harriet," said Alexa, walking past in a black pair of trousers and a black vest top. "One *hundred and fifty* per cent. So don't you worry either."

And she gives me a sly wink and disappears into a dark corner.

I suddenly feel dizzy.

"That's not possible," I murmur under my breath. "It

only goes up to a hundred per cent. That's the whole point of the expression."

Then I swallow.

Ten years of memories of Alexa are suddenly racing back at once. A decade of humiliation: of pointing, of laughing, of ripping me apart. Now she's got the power to do it all unseen. In front of the whole school.

And teachers.

And my parents.

I twitch the curtain slightly and stare out at the crowd. Every seat in the room is full, and everyone is starting to quieten down. The lights have dipped, and there's a hush descending.

Apart from in my dad's corner, obviously. He's stuffing a piece of pizza in his mouth and loudly asking, "What happens at the end of Romeo and Juliet?".

I swallow and grab the paper bag from Nat.

"OK?" she whispers at me, as Miss Hammond lines everybody up against the wall behind the stage and holds her fingers over her lips.

"Yup," I lie. "Brilliant."

"Now," Miss Hammond says with a jangle of a crushing weight of bangles: she must have very strong arm muscles. "Let the magic begin."

28

Now, I know quite a lot about magic.

I know that the word *magic* is derived from the Persian word *magus*, which means 'one of the priestly class'. I know that 'the bullet catch' has killed twelve magicians, and that the most expensive magic show cost £20.8 million to stage.

I know that I've tried a range of *Harry Potter* spells to open doors, create light and repair things I've broken, and not a single one of them has ever worked.

But I'm starting to think maybe I don't know *everything*.

Because as the curtain rises smoothly and the ghost of Hamlet Senior walks solemnly on to the stage, there's definitely *some* kind of enchantment going on.

Everything is perfect.

Ghostly blue light is shining directly upon him. A distant owl is hooting; the trees Year 9 art class made are fake-rustling from a stereo in the corner. The crowd is silent.

Everyone and everything is exactly where it's supposed to be.

"Long live the King!" Hannah shouts. "Look where it comes again, in the same figure like the King that's dead. Thou art a scholar – speak to it, Horatio."

And, line by line, the play starts unfolding flawlessly.

Noah's ghost is fearful and demanding; Ben's King Claudius is repulsive and creepy; Kira's Queen Gertrude

has a terrifying edge that brings a whole other level to the play.

Hannah manages to seamlessly blend four roles, and Raya's wobbly, tear-stricken performance is so genuine that at one point somebody in the audience starts sniffling into a tissue and mumbling, "Poor, poor Ophelia."

"My lord," she tells Polonius earnestly, "he hath importuned me with love in honourable fashion."

Her voice breaks.

"He *did*," she ad-libs, a real tear rolling down her cheek. "He really, really *did*. He was so *lovely*."

In the meantime, Hamlet stomps around the stage wearing a black cloak and flinging his arms around a lot.

"Owww *dude*," the ghost of his father mutters as he gets accidentally smacked in the face. "Calm it down, buddy, or you're going to get thumped."

Finally, I feel a gentle hand on my arm and I know it's my turn.

"Good luck," Nat whispers, squeezing my shoulder.

And I clench my sweaty palms together and walk on to the stage.

I blink in the lights a few times.

Somewhere in the distance, I can see Dad standing up with his video camera light flashing.

I try to ignore it and take a deep breath.

"God save you, sir," I say as clearly as I can.

An *apocaholic* is a person obsessed with the possibility of imminent disaster, and I think that can definitely describe me right now: every muscle in my body feels like it's made out of galvanised rubber.

Silence.

"What make you at Elsinore?" Christopher asks, patting me stiffly on the shoulder.

I swallow and glance to the left, where I can vaguely see the dim outline of Alexa sitting by the music system. She seems to be focusing intently on a magazine in front of her and paying no attention to us at all.

"To visit you, my lord," I say, starting to relax slightly. "No other occasion."

"I know the King and Queen have sent for you."

I can feel my neck starting to soften, then my shoulders, then the top of my arms. "To what end, my lord?"

"That *you* must teach *me*. If you love me, hold not off."

Everything in my body slowly starts to unwind. "My lord, we *were* sent for."

"I will tell you *why*," Hamlet snaps moodily, and then throws his arms in the air and launches into a long and kind of unprovoked monologue all about canopies of air and a majestic roof fretted with golden fire.

I blink a few times as he pounds around the stage and look around the room in shock.

Have I done it?

Have I actually managed to get through a scene without ruining anything, breaking anything, forcing anyone to fall over or destroying the entire show in the process?

More importantly, did Alexa just *let* me?

There are about 700 muscles in the human body, and every one of mine suddenly melts until it's warm and floppy.

I did! I *did* it!

Beaming, I glance at Nat, standing in the shadows

behind the curtains, and subtly stick my thumbs in the air. Then I start mentally preparing myself for my final line.

"What a piece of work is a man," Christopher continues, charging to the right of the stage. "How noble in reason, how infinite in faculties, in form and moving how express and admirable." He charges to the left. "In action how like an angel, in apprehension how like a god!"

A dog barks.

Christopher pauses in confusion. "I said how like a *god*," he says crossly. "Not a *dog*."

Then he turns to me.

I'm still staring off stage, wondering vaguely if somebody's brought a pet with them.

"It's your turn," Christopher reminds me aggressively under his breath. Then he turns back to the audience and shouts again, "How like a god!"

"Oh," I say, blinking at him. "Umm, my lord, there was no—"

A lion roars.

"Th-there was no…" A cat meows. "No…"

The lights turn on and off; the crowd has started giggling. My entire head has emptied completely, like an upturned penny jar.

Just pick the next line you can remember, Harriet. "To think, my lord, that—"

Cheep cheep. Ribbit. Cockadoodle do.

"That—"

Oink oink. The lights flash a few more times. *Oink.*

The students in the audience are starting to laugh loudly now, and one quick glance to the side confirms it: Alexa's face is a picture of innocence.

Which means it's totally her.

People are starting to clap, parents are starting to mumble at each other and Miss Hammond is crouch-running like a hobbit across the floor in front of the stage to get to the other side as quickly as possible.

Christopher's face is going steadily purple.

"If you…" I stutter. "If you, umm…"

And then I hear it. With everybody's full attention on the stage, the volume suddenly gets a little louder.

"Harriet Manners *stinks*," a familiar voice booms from the speaker as a bright white light settles on my head.

Every single blood vessel in my body feels like it's draining into my feet.

Where do I know that from?

Oh my God: the *cheese*. It wasn't just planted there to ruin my morning – Alexa was *recording* the class on her phone.

"I…" I stutter. "I…"

There's a type of pygmy seahorse that is virtually indistinguishable from the coral it lives in. At this precise moment, I'd give anything for that kind of camouflage.

Or just being tiny enough to become invisible.

Every single pair of eyes in the room is now focused on me.

"Uh," I manage, then there's a burst of disco music as red and green and blue lights start pulsing.

And Hamlet finally has enough.

"*I will not tolerate this*," Christopher yells, ripping the crown off his head and throwing it on to the floor. "*This is MY PLAY. I'm the PRINCE OF FLAMING DENMARK*."

And before I can stop him, with one smooth gesture,

Christopher flings his cloak over his shoulder, jumps off the stage and flounces out of the hall.

Leaving me, alone and flashing like a smelly rainbow, on the stage behind him.

29

There's a long silence.

The kind of silence you could drink, should you be interested in drinking silences.

Then two hundred eyes spin back round and focus on me. I can feel the heat from my cheeks steadily making its way into my ears, my throat, my neck, my eyes.

"Umm," I say slowly, getting hotter and hotter. "Well. Right."

This is worse than I could possibly have expected. Alexa hasn't just destroyed me this time. She's destroyed everyone else and the entire play in the process.

When I glance to the side, she's already disappeared. I think Christopher's extreme diva reaction was a bit of a surprise, even for her.

"Err," I bleat nervously as the silence continues to stretch on. *Quick, Harriet. Don't let her win.* "Goodness me, how stressedeth out Hamlet is these days." I flush a bit harder. *Stressedeth out?* "By my word, he is mad north-north west. So, umm…"

A heckler from the crowd makes an *oink oink* sound.

"I don't get it," one of the parents mumbles audibly. "Is it a post modern version or something?"

"So," I continue in a trembling voice, "uh, why don't we… umm… have a little break while Hamlet gets his head together and then…"

And I falter to an abrupt stop.

How on earth are you supposed to perform *Hamlet* without Hamlet? It's like going to McDonald's and ordering a salad.

"Wooooo!" I hear my dad shout supportively from the back. "This play is thoroughly excellent and I am very much enjoying this pretty redhead's acting."

That totally didn't make it worse at all.

"You could all go for a cup of tea while Hamlet calms down," I suggest, going slightly redder. "Or a coffee." That's it: I've lost my head. This hydra has totally disintegrated. "Maybe some biscuits, chocolate ones. Or…"

"OK," Mr Bott says gently, stepping out from behind the curtains as I go into verbal meltdown. "Thank you, Harriet." He turns to the audience. "We'll have to call it a day on this performance, I'm afraid. I'm sure you'll all be thrilled to hear that the government are considering taking Shakespeare off the syllabus in the near future."

"I'm not sure about this school," somebody mutters at the front. "That wasn't how I remember Kenneth Branagh's version."

Suddenly – in the middle of the confused murmuring – there's a voice from the side. A voice I know well.

Possibly too well.

"To be or not to be," it says loudly. "That *is* the question."

And a skinny boy in a red T-shirt with *THIS SHIRT IS BLUE IF YOU RUN FAST ENOUGH* written on it in large letters walks up the stairs on to the stage.

"Whether 'tis nobler in the mind to suffer the slings and arrows of outrageous fortune," he continues, "or to take arms against a sea of trouble and by opposing end them."

"*Toby*?" I say in astonishment.

"Or *not* Toby," he says, looking very pleased with himself. "That is another very good question, Harriet. Hahaha."

Then he looks back at the audience and continues the speech easily. There's no intonation in his voice at all – he sounds like a robot – but every word is perfect.

The crowd has gone totally silent, and some of them have started sitting back down again.

I look at Mr Bott.

It's the wrong bit of the play – Toby's skipped right ahead to the next act – but it doesn't actually make a lot of difference in Miss Hammond's 'free jazz' version.

Mr Bott shrugs, makes a go for it gesture with his hand and steps back behind the curtains.

"Oh, Hamlet," I say woodenly. "How, umm, nice of you to come back with a different, err, face and outfit."

"I'm the Dr Who of Shakespearean heroes, Rosencrantz-hyphen-Guildenstern, who, for the record, does not smell at all," Toby says, nodding. "For who would bear the whips and scorns of time…"

Still blinking, I mentally scan through the play in my head. I'm not in this bit: it's Hamlet and Ophelia. So I run off the stage and quickly grab a blinking Raya.

"What's going on?" she sniffles into her tissue.

"Act three, scene one," I say as I gently push her on to the stage. "Good my lord, etcetera."

"Oh," she says, still looking confused. Then she straightens her shoulders and lifts her chin. "Good my lord," she says to Toby, and her bewilderment is absolutely perfect, "how does your honour for this many a day?"

And the play begins again in earnest, except this time Hamlet doesn't punch anybody in the face, kiss anyone or throw a wobbler and jump off the stage.

Of all the people in the world who might know a Shakespearean play without actually being given a part, it would definitely be Toby.

Or Kenneth Branagh. Obviously.

I slip behind the darkened curtain, and then look at the space where Alexa was a few minutes ago. Instead, Miss Hammond is standing there with her arms crossed.

"*So* many detentions," she says, with an expression I've never seen on her face before. "I am quite, *quite* furious."

And as she storms off, necklaces tinkling, I suddenly go very still.

Alexa is standing silently in the dark, with her hands wrapped around the curtain ropes. She hasn't seen me, but is obviously not done yet, and frankly – after ten years of knowing her – I can't believe I thought for a second she might be.

To be, or not to be. That is the question.

Whether 'tis nobler in the mind to suffer the slings and arrows of outrageous fortune or to take arms against a sea of trouble and by opposing end them.

There's a word for an inability to make decisions: it's called *abulia*.

That's what *Hamlet* is really about, isn't it?

Choosing to stand up against your enemies, or not. Choosing to fight back, or to duck your head and just put up with it. And the ultimate lesson is: the longer you fail to make a choice, one way or another, the more damage is done.

The more people get hurt.

So, in that split second, I make mine.

"Hello," I say calmly as Alexa starts tugging on the rope and the curtain directly above Toby starts gradually inching downwards.

She smiles smugly.

"Hello, geek," she says back. "This is such a fun play, isn't it?" She grins and pulls on the curtain rope. "I *did* tell you I'd always be behind you."

"You did," I say, leaning forward and pulling open a door slightly to the left of her. "But do you know what that logically means, Alexa?"

"What?"

I put a hand gently on her shoulder. "It means I'll always be in front."

Alexa looks in amazement at my hand.

"Excuse me, but are you actually *touching* me?" she splutters in shock. "Like, with your real fingers? What do you think you're *doing*?"

"I'm taking arms against a sea of trouble," I say calmly, pushing her firmly back a few metres. "And by opposing, ending them."

Then, as Alexa stares at me with her mouth open and a torrent of cutting words about to tumble from her lips, I firmly swing the door in front of her face.

And lock her in the cupboard.

30

The rest of the play goes as follows:

- Toby kills Polonius, attacks the Queen, shouts at his King, dumps Ophelia and fights Laertes.
- Toby sends out orders to have me killed.
- Then apologises profusely in a loudly improvised piece about how awesome I am.
- Ophelia cries herself into a sleepy stupor and then drowns herself on a big blue sheet dragged grumpily across the stage by Hannah.
- The ghost gets caught kissing Horatio behind the curtain.

There's also quite a fun moment where a sharp voice announces from the audience:

"Is that my *wedding* dress, Natalie Grey?"

Followed by a sigh and: "Oh, well. It wasn't that lucky first time round either, poor girl."

(Nat's dad ran off with the checkout girl from Sainsbury's.)

By the time my best friend has fluffed up her hair and laid down on the floor with her face pointing awkwardly towards the audience, I think everyone is really starting to enjoy themselves.

You can tell, because the audience has started loudly supporting their favourite characters as if it's a football match.

124

"You go, Hamlet!" one shouts.

"Horatio, I love you!"

"Where's the ghost gone? He's super hot."

Toby remains completely impervious to the attention he's getting. I guess there are some benefits to being socially oblivious, after all.

"Alas," he says calmly, kneeling on the floor and prodding Nat's face. "Poor Yorick. I knew him, Horatio."

Nat abruptly jumps up, and I wince and put my hands over my eyes.

Sugar cookies.

"Yes," she says loudly. "But I've been dead in the cold, cold ground for many years now, and I will never see the warm light of the sun again. I'm so cold. So very, very cold. It's so sad. Remember me. Remember *meeeee*."

And – as I peek through my fingers – Nat does a little bow and lies calmly back down in her grave again.

"Yeeeahhh!" Dad yells out. "Go Yorick! You rock, girl!"

I relax with relief. OK: that's nowhere near as bad as I thought it would be. The hamster is safe, after all.

From behind the curtains, Hannah, Noah and I give each other a nod and then start hauling Raya back on to the stage, while Hamlet and Laertes yell at each other about who is most upset about her death.

Then we place her in the middle of the stage and stand respectfully to the side while she's buried.

Or, you know. Is supposed to be.

"I loved Ophelia!" Toby says stiffly, bending down and touching Raya's hand. "Forty thousand brothers could not have—"

Raya's eyes snap open. "No, you didn't."

There's a pause. "Sorry?"

"You didn't love me *at all*." She sits up with her hair sticking out vertically and her eyelids swollen and pink like thick bits of ham. "You *said* you did, but you didn't. It was all rubbish."

"But I *did* love you," Toby says in consternation. "It says so in the script."

"No," Ophelia snaps, her voice getting louder and louder. "You just like *saying* it. It doesn't *mean* anything to you. You go on and on about your feelings because it makes you feel like a hero, but that's not real *love*. Love is, like, *not* killing somebody's dad, for starters."

"I'm terribly sorry about that," Toby admits. "It was a pretty big error of judgement."

"And love is *not* dumping someone and then trying to send them to a nunnery so they can't meet anyone else."

"Agreed," Toby says. "That is very true."

"And love is *not* asking out that dimwit in your art class who I asked you time and time again if you liked and you said no and you were obviously *lying* because I saw the text on your phone!"

"Umm." Toby looks completely startled. "Yes, well. Indeed."

There's a muscle twitching in the corner of Raya's mouth, and her eyes are shining. "So stop thinking about yourself all the time," she snaps angrily, "and show me some *respect*."

She lies back down again with her hands crossed neatly over her front like a vampire and closes her eyes.

There's a hushed silence.

Then somebody in the audience yells: "*Do* something, Hammers!"

"Don't be such a douchebag, Hamlet!"

"Girl power, Ophelia!" somebody cries from behind the curtains, and it sounds suspiciously like Miss Hammond.

Toby frowns and looks round the stage. We're all watching him anxiously.

"You've made a series of very valid points, Ophelia," he says after a thoughtful pause. "So, as you're clearly alive, shall we get married and forget about this revenge business?"

Ophelia sits up and wipes her eyes. "Yeah, go on then."

"Does this mean I don't die?" Laertes checks.

"Or me?" says Claudius.

"And I don't have to lie on the floor?" Gertrude asks. "Because frankly it's totally filthy."

"Nobody dies at all!" Toby says jubilantly. "It's all going to be OK!"

"Apart from me," the ghost of Hamlet's father points out gloomily. "I'm still dead, right?"

"And me," Polonius points out. "Figures."

Everybody grins at each other.

This is definitely the way *Hamlet* should have gone. I mean, it worked for *Much Ado About Nothing*, didn't it? And *Romeo and Juliet* would have been a lot more cheerful if Juliet had sat up on her deathbed and yelled at Romeo for being an idiot just ten minutes earlier.

"Right," Toby says cheerfully, holding out what appears to be a yellow jelly sweet ring. "It's a good thing I keep these in my pocket."

And as Ophelia jumps up, sorts out her dress and the

funeral vicar conducts a hurried and totally ad-libbed marriage service, the crowd stands up and starts cheering.

Maybe a happy ending is what everyone is really looking for, after all.

31

By the time we've taken our seventh group bow of the evening and various parents start congratulating Mr Bott on an "inspirational interpretation that really questions *genre*, doesn't it?" I'm so flushed with success I've almost forgotten what I have to do now.

Almost, but not quite.

As the curtain closes for the final time, I hold on to Nat's hand for just a bit longer than I have to.

Her face is glowing, and she's glancing up and down the row of cast members with a distracted, critical eye. "Should have given Mia the flat cap," she murmurs to herself. "And Raya's shoes needed to have softer soles. Maybe a ballet pump, or a low-heeled Mary-Jane, or—"

"Nat," I say quickly, squeezing her hand. It's so clear now, I can't believe I didn't see it before.

Except – as with the stilton – maybe we don't notice what's right under our noses.

"You should still go into fashion. But as a designer or a stylist or something. You'd be perfect at it."

Nat frowns.

"But it's really competitive, Harriet," she says doubtfully, "and I'm not sure I—"

"It doesn't matter. You love it and you're incredibly talented. Think about it?"

Nat nods and blinks a few times, and I squeeze her

hand and jump off the stage.

Toby is calmly explaining his T-shirt to a group of parents clustered enthusiastically around him.

"It's red now," he's saying, pulling at his own sleeve, "but if I was to run very fast it would compress the frequency of the light waves and therefore become blue. It's called the Doppler effect."

He starts running around in a circle a few times to demonstrate.

"Sadly, though," he adds, "I would have to move at approximately 340 million miles an hour, and, given my current PE grades, that seems unlikely."

I tap him on the shoulder.

"Umm," I say anxiously, clearing my throat, "Toby, I think you saved the play."

"Probably," Toby agrees, sticking his finger in his ear, digging around for a few seconds and then wiping it on his trousers. "I was just relieved I didn't have to step in as Ophelia."

I laugh. That would have been a very postmodern interpretation of *Hamlet*. Miss Hammond would have been delighted.

"Well," I say. "Thank you."

And – before I can stop myself – I throw my arms loosely around his skinny chest and give him a tentative hug.

"Does this mean we're going out now?" he checks.

I grin and start heading backstage again. The heart is situated just to the left of the breastbone, and you can say what you like about Toby, but his is definitely in the right place.

"Nope," I call over my shoulder. "But maybe next time

you're at my house, knock on the door instead of hiding in the bushes."

Finally, I reach the darkest corner of backstage and stop.

I take a deep breath.

I take another one, because I think I'm going to need it.

Then, like Lucy about to confront the White Witch of Narnia, I cautiously take a step forward.

And open the door of the cupboard.

32

Apparently, fewer than four people a year are killed by sharks. Statistically, they are less dangerous than lightning, cows, coconuts and foods with high saturated fat contents.

I still know which one I wouldn't go swimming with, though.

Let's just say: some endings are scarier than others.

"*You*," Alexa hisses coldly, narrowing her eyes. "*You*."

I nod. "Me," I agree.

Miss Hammond appears from around the corner. Her necklaces are jangling so hard she sounds like an approaching sleigh pulled by a team of hyperactive reindeer.

"*Alexa*," she says loudly, "I want to see you in my office *right now*."

She doesn't have an office – she's a drama teacher – but that's not a clarification I'm going to make.

Alexa rolls her eyes and then glares at me.

"I'm going to make you pay for locking me in a cupboard," she snarls under her breath. "Believe me, Harriet. You've just made your life five trillion times harder. This isn't over."

"Obviously," I say, watching as she's marched out of the room with Miss Hammond behind her.

The doors swing shut just as my bottom starts vibrating. For a second, I'm so distracted I think I might have turned into a bumblebee.

Then I remember I popped my phone into my back trouser pocket in the last scene, just in case of emergencies.

Or – you know.

So Australian boys can call me.

"Hey," a warm voice says. "Is it done? Was it great? Did you smash it?" Then there's a laugh. "Actually, you might literally have smashed it. You didn't destroy the entire set, did you?"

The heart might normally be red, but mine is suddenly beating so fast there's a really good chance it's now bright blue.

I smile and stand behind the curtains so I can watch the happy chaos unfold.

The entire room is bright and full of noise.

Raya is pink cheeked and talking to a good-looking boy in Year 12; Max and Ben are fencing each other with two stolen mops; Hannah is playing Rock-Paper-Scissors with Rob. Kira is being reluctantly hugged by two teary-eyed adults, and Christopher is regaling everyone with anecdotes about his *dramatic* process.

Mia and Noah are sitting with their fingertips touching.

Even Mr Bott has his arms unfolded, possibly for the first time in known history.

Everyone looks so proud. So excited. So happy.

"It was brilliant," I say in surprise as Dad starts trying to film the pizza box and Annabel tries to stop him. "Kind of... fun, actually."

I can't promise I'll ever be in a play again – unless I'm cast as a silent potato, or maybe a piece of watermelon – but I think I was wrong.

Maybe drama can be quite cathartic after all.

"So I'll pop over tomorrow and watch the full, unedited video with you?"

I think about the dogs barking, the cats meowing, the cockerels crowing. I think about the rainbow lights and disco music; my apparent smelliness. My inexplicable offering of biscuits to a hundred total strangers.

My total, public humiliation.

"Sure," I smile. If Nick's going to hang out with me, he might as well know what he's getting himself into. "See you tomorrow."

Then I put down the phone and look at Nat.

She's in the corner of the room, animatedly showing her mum the yellow buttons she sewed on to Rob's velvet jacket. Her cheeks are pink, her eyes are shining and her hands are moving at a mile a minute, which is what happens when she's really, really excited about something.

They say there's an invisible tie between you and the people you love. For just a few seconds I can feel it running from me to my best friend and back again.

Nat must be able to feel it too.

Because, in the middle of a sentence, she stops, looks up and winks at me.

I wink back.

And it suddenly doesn't matter what Alexa has in store for me. It doesn't matter how bad it's going to get.

There's always somebody holding my hand.

So I won't have to face it alone.

Read more from Geek Girl...

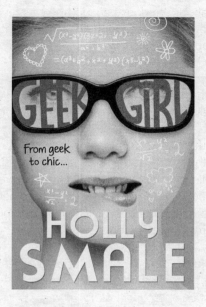

Harriet Manners knows a lot of things.

✶ Cats have 32 muscles in each ear.
✶ Bluebirds can't see the colour blue.
✶ The average person laughs 15 times per day.
✶ Peanuts are an ingredient of dynamite.

But she doesn't know why nobody at school seems to like her. So when she's offered the chance to reinvent herself, Harriet grabs it. Can she transform from geek to chic?

And get your geek on with Harriet Manners as she jets off to Tokyo and New York...

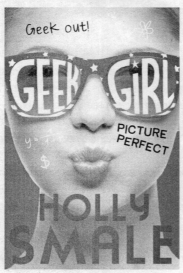

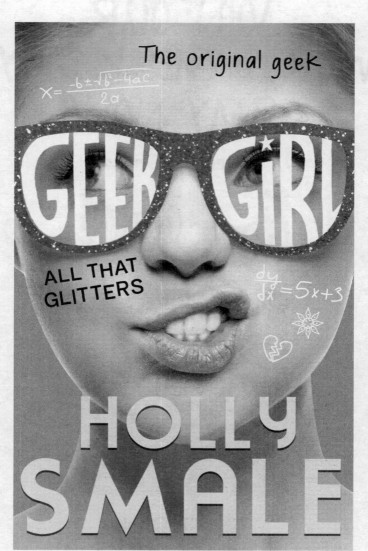

JOIN OUR
WORLD GEEK DAY
ARMY NOW!

f /GeekGirlSeries

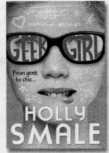

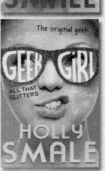

 @HolSmale

#worldgeekday   #worldbookday

WORLD BOOK DAY 5 MARCH 2015

WORLD BOOK DAY *fest*

A BIG, HAPPY, BOOKY CELEBRATION OF READING

» Want to READ more? «

VISIT your local bookshop

- Get some great recommendations for what to read next
- Meet your favourite authors & illustrators at brilliant events
- Discover books you never even knew existed!

FIND YOUR LOCAL BOOKSHOP www.booksellers.org.uk/bookshopsearch

JOIN your local library

You can browse and borrow from a HUGE selection of books and get recommendations of what to read next from expert librarians—all for **FREE**! You can also discover libraries' wonderful children's and family reading activities.

FIND YOUR LOCAL LIBRARY www.findalibrary.co.uk

Get ONLINE!

Visit WORLDBOOKDAY.COM to discover a whole new world of books!

- Downloads and activities for **FAB** books and authors
- Cool games, trailers and videos
- Author events in your area
- News, competitions and new books —all in a **FREE** monthly email

and MORE!

AND HARPERCOLLINS CHILDREN'S BOOKS

PRESENTS ANOTHER AMAZING READ...

BY

SOMAN CHAINANI

1

The Princess & The Witch

Sophie had waited all her life to be kidnapped.

But tonight, all the other children of Gavaldon writhed in their beds. If the School Master took them, they'd never return. Never lead a full life. Never see their family again. Tonight these children dreamt of a red-eyed thief with the body of a beast, come to rip them from their sheets and stifle their screams.

Sophie dreamt of princes instead.

She had arrived at a castle ball thrown in her honor, only to find the hall filled with a hundred suitors and no other girls in sight. Here for the first time were boys who deserved her, she thought as she walked the line. Hair shiny and thick, muscles taut through shirts, skin smooth and tan, beautiful and attentive like princes should be. But just as she came to one who seemed better than the rest, with brilliant blue eyes and ghostly white hair, the one who felt like Happily Ever After . . . a hammer broke through the walls of the room and smashed the princes to shards.

Sophie's eyes opened to morning. The hammer was real. The princes were not.

"Father, if I don't sleep nine hours, my eyes look swollen."

"Everyone's prattling on that you're to be taken this year," her father said, nailing a misshapen bar over her bedroom window, now completely obscured by locks, spikes, and screws. "They tell me to shear your hair, muddy up your face, as if I believe all this fairy-tale hogwash. But no one's getting in here tonight. That's for sure." He pounded a deafening crack as exclamation.

Sophie rubbed her ears and frowned at her once lovely window, now something you'd see in a witch's den. "Locks. Why didn't anyone think of that before?"

"I don't know why they all think it's you," he said, silver hair slicked with sweat. "If it's goodness that School Master fellow wants, he'll take Gunilda's daughter."

Sophie tensed. "Belle?"

"Perfect child that one is," he said. "Brings her father home-cooked lunches at the mill. Gives the leftovers to the poor hag in the square."

Sophie heard the edge in her father's voice. She had never once cooked a full meal for him, even after her mother died. Naturally she had good reason (the oil and smoke would clog her pores) but she knew it was a sore point. This didn't mean her father had gone hungry. Instead, she offered him her own favorite foods: mashed beets, broccoli stew, boiled asparagus, steamed spinach. He hadn't ballooned into a blimp like Belle's father, precisely because she hadn't brought him home-cooked lamb fricassees and cheese soufflés at the mill. As for the poor hag in the square, that old crone, despite claiming hunger day after day, was *fat*. And if Belle had anything to do with it, then she wasn't good at all, but the worst kind of evil.

Sophie smiled back at her father. "Like you said, it's all hogwash." She swept out of bed and slammed the bathroom door.

She studied her face in the mirror. The rude awakening had taken its toll. Her waist-long hair, the color of spun gold, didn't have its usual sheen. Her jade-green eyes looked faded, her luscious red lips a touch dry. Even the glow of her creamy peach skin had dulled. *But still a princess*, she thought. Her father couldn't see she was special, but her mother had. "You are too beautiful for this world, Sophie," she said with her last breaths. Her mother had gone somewhere better and now so would she.

Tonight she would be taken into the woods. Tonight she would begin a new life. Tonight she would live out her fairy tale.

And now she needed to look the part.

To begin, she rubbed fish eggs into her skin, which smelled of dirty feet but warded off spots. Then she massaged in pumpkin puree, rinsed with goat's milk, and soaked her face in a mask of melon and turtle egg yolk. As she waited for the mask to dry, Sophie flipped through a storybook and sipped on cucumber juice to keep her skin dewy soft. She skipped to her favorite part of the story, where the wicked hag is rolled down a hill in a nail-spiked barrel, until all that remains is her bracelet made of little boys' bones. Gazing at the gruesome bracelet, Sophie felt her thoughts drift to cucumbers. Suppose there were no cucumbers in the woods? Suppose other princesses had depleted the supply?

No cucumbers! She'd shrivel, she'd wither, she'd—

Dried melon flakes fell to the page. She turned to the mirror and saw her brow creased in worry. First ruined sleep and now wrinkles. At this rate she'd be a hag by afternoon. She relaxed her face and banished thoughts of vegetables.

As for the rest of Sophie's beauty routine, it could fill a dozen storybooks (suffice it to say it included goose feathers, pickled potatoes, horse hooves, cream of cashews, and a vial of cows' blood). Two hours of rigorous grooming later, she stepped from the house in a breezy pink dress, sparkling glass heels, and hair in an impeccable braid. She had one last day before the School Master's arrival and planned to use each and every minute to remind him why she, and not Belle or Tabitha or Sabrina or any other impostor, should be kidnapped.

GET THE BOOK TO READ MORE...

ISBN 9780007492930